A HARVARD
EDUCATION
IN A BOOK

A HARVARD EDUCATION IN A BOOK

by the Editors of

THE HARVARD LAMPOON

A PERIGEE BOOK

We dedicate this book to the Motor City Madman, Ted Nugent: By
never compromising, never selling out, never betraying your gift for
the seductive yet empty rewards of commercial success, you have
inspired an entire generation of young humorists.
The book is also dedicated to Johnny Winter, our parents, and
Alice Cooper.

Perigee Books
are published by
The Putnam Publishing Group
200 Madison Avenue
New York, NY 10016

Published simultaneously in Canada

Library of Congress Cataloging-in-Publication Data

A Harvard education in a book / by the editors of The Harvard lampoon.
p. cm.
1. Harvard University—Humor. 2. Education, Higher—United
States—Humor. I. Harvard lampoon.
PN6231.S3H37 1991 91-12576 CIP
378.744′4—dc20
ISBN 0-399-51665-4 (trade pbk.)
Cover design by Paul Bacon

Printed in the United States of America
1 2 3 4 5 6 7 8 9 10

This book is printed on acid-free paper.
∞

PHOTO CREDITS

Adam D. Galinsky—A Word From Your Professors, Garbology, Tools, the photo of the authors, Dream Potty

Lisa J. Borodkin—Photo tour pictures on pages 17, 19, 20, 21, 22, 23

Alec H. Berg—Famous Harvard Grads, Photo tour pictures on pages 18, 20, 21

Stephen R. Meyer—Anxiety

Daniel T. Pereira—McDonald's

David Van—Swim Test

BOOK STAFF

Editor: Jon D. Beckerman
Staff Writers: Robinson O. Everett, Matthew C. Moehlman, Daniel J. O'Keefe, Brian D. Reich, Jeffrey C. Schaffer
Additional Contributors: Alexander H. Berg, Ronald E. Corcillo, Allen Glazier
Staff Artist: Adam J.B. Lane
Additional Artists: Jon D. Beckerman, Daniel Chung
Photographers: Alexander H. Berg, Lisa J. Borodkin, Adam D. Galinsky, Stephen R. Meyer, Daniel T. Pereira, David Van
Oh, yeah, and don't forget . . .: Maya C.M.I. Forbes

THE HARVARD LAMPOON

Board of Editors: Alison G. Umminger '92 (President), David P. Lorsch '92 (Ibis), Stephen R. Meyer '91–'92 (Narthex), Matthew C. Moehlman '92 (Narthex), Lewis N. Morton '93 (Sackbut), Justin P. Monge '92 (Hautbois), Adam J.B. Lane '93 (Sanctum), Vanessa Ward '92 (Librarian), Jon D. Beckerman '91, Michael A. Mattison '91, Elijah F. Aron '92–93, Brian D. Reich '91, Ravin K. R. Agrawal '91, Laurence C. O'Keefe '91, Erich Fox Tree '91, Jeffrey C. Schaffer '91, John M. Barker '91–'92, J. Stewart Burns '92, Andrew Oliver '92, Alexander H. Berg '91, Michael A. Green '91, Seth K. Jacobson '91–

'92, Jonathan D. Baird '92, Sean P. Kelly '92, Daniel Chung '93, David H. Mandel '92, Linda M. Rattner '92, Matthew R. Grenby '93, David Javerbaum '93, David J. Kennedy '93, Richard L. Levy '93, Steven G. Lookner '93, Elisabeth J. Sedano '93, Merrill Kaplan '94

Business Editors: Ruben N. Lubowski '92 (Treasurer), Daniel T. Pereira '92 (Business Manager), Alexandra Maggioni '92 (Business Manager), Jocelyn C. Stamat '92 (Circulation Manager), Joseph N. Locke '92 (Distribution Manager), Lance P.D. Khazei '89–'91, Justin V. Graham '92, Steven L. Karan '91, Stefan G. Wathne '91, Justin H. Gordon '92, Karen D. Snyder '92

Grand Generalissimo: Elmer W. Green, 1897–1977

CONTENTS

HARVARD MAN

III. LET'S LEARN TOGETHER!

$E=MC^2$

IV. NOW WHAT?

BUT I'VE *BEEN* TO HARTFORD
OR
WHY DO I NEED THIS BOOK?

A Rude Welcome from the Editors of the *Harvard Lampoon*

You're not alone. Like hundreds of people worldwide, you didn't go to Harvard College. That's because a Harvard education is something that society has reserved for an ultra-exclusive, tiny elite group of wealthy intellectuals. So what can the *Harvard Lampoon* do about it? Well, we can't make you wealthy; only crime can do that. And we can't raise your intelligence; that would require surgery and a lifetime of exposure to the proper flash cards.

As a matter of fact, we can't even get you into Harvard. It seems like every time we recommend someone for admission we hear about their "suicide" on the next morning's news. But (and here's where things start looking up) we *can* give you everything that Harvard has to offer, short of a place to hide for four years. We can give you the knowledge. The social grace. The personal enrichment. *And the diploma, even the goddamn diploma.* It's right there on page 183, suitable for framing! And all this for less than you lose in five minutes at the cock fights.

Perhaps this doesn't interest you. *Ahhhh, Harvard Shmarvard,* you say. Well then, maybe you can tell us how come 2 million applicants practically eat each other to get the sixteen hundred spots in each year's freshman class? How come each of those sixteen hundred chosen ones is so thankful that he stops kissing his guidance counselor's butt long enough to stand up and hand him the keys to a new luxury sedan? How come Harvard grads get the best jobs, the ones in which all the work is done by computers willing to let them take all the credit? *How come Harvard is kicking ass all over the map?*

13

We're not trying to put you on the spot—these are the questions that keep us *Harvard students* awake at night. We just want to *help* you. We understand that people out there in the real world can't just say, "Boss, gimme some vacation time. I need to enrich myself at the finest undergraduate institution in the country." Because if they do, the boss will just say, "Shut up and get back to the Pollution Machine, Number 433288!"

The point is that if you were really going to Harvard, you'd be in a car now, towing a U-Haul full of spiral notebooks to Cambridge, Massachusetts. You'd be looking back on memories of teenage years spent making straight A's, editing the school paper, running the student council, and still finding time to teach latch-key kids how to make God's-eyes. But thanks to us, you can stay at home, look back on a lifetime of being a goof, and *still* get a Harvard education.

We're not just trying to sell a book here—although selling a book would not suck. We're trying to create a Utopia. And not a Utopia where some big robot is in charge and everyone else gets screwed. In fact, not any of the bad Utopias for which the literature has prepared us, but instead a *good* Utopia in which education is as available as genital warts and just as difficult to avoid.

Welcome to our Utopia, dear reader, a Utopia where everyone has a Harvard education. In our land, "I" and "the" are no longer the most commonly used English words. They have long been overtaken by "sherry," "Nietzsche," and "I can march into any office in the world, demand a job, and be made executive vice-president on the spot." Get it?

You are about to embark on the greatest educational adventure of your lifetime, and the only thing that's holding you back is this introduction. But for no longer.

Turn the page, *freshman.*

Part
I

WELCOME TO HARVARD!

A PHOTO TOUR OF HARVARD YARD
(NEVER MIND THE GORILLA)

Welcome to beautiful Harvard Yard!

Harvard Yard is where freshman live and where most classes are held. It is also pretty famous, although there is not much for visitors to see except some drab old buildings and a couple of patches of ill-kept grass. Tourists who come planning to "pahk the cah in Hahvahd Yahd" are in for an additional disappointment, as there is only one parking space and it is reserved for the handicapped.

Still, if you want to get a feel for what "The Harvard Experience" is like, you should at least look at some pictures of the place, provided you have nothing better to do. To simulate the experience of taking a tour as closely as possible, you may want to stare off into space, think your own thoughts, and fish pebbles out of your shoes instead of paying attention.

This is the famous Widener Library, dedicated to the memory of Harry Elkins Widener, a Harvard student who drowned in a swimming pool aboard the *Titanic*. The building was donated by his parents, who had no use for it. The Wideners' gift stipulated that their son's collection of "private" magazines should be stored under some socks in the bottom-right drawer of a dresser, just like he had kept them. It also demanded that the building must never be altered from its original design, and that "should even one brick be removed from the building, ownership of the library will immediately revert to the city of Cambridge."

Rising to a height of 10,000 feet, Harvard's statue of its founder, John Harvard, towers over the entire Boston metropolitan area and is visible from a major portion of New England. (To give some sense of perspective, a dollar bill that is 1,000 times the length of an ordinary dollar has been taped to the statue.) The John Harvard statue has been dubbed the "Statue of the Three Lies" because the 3 legends engraved on its base are all false. The first lie is that the statue labels John Harvard as the college's "Founder" when, in fact, the Massachusetts government founded Harvard. The second lie is that the statue says Harvard was "Founded in 1638," when it was really 1636. The statue's third lie is, "There are only two lies engraved on this statue."

This guardhouse, standing at the gate to Harvard Yard, is notorious for having cost over $200,000 to build. Those who have seen only its modest exterior often question the expense, but any who have been inside to see the many sumptuously furnished rooms and priceless works of art do not. In fact, the guards' sole function is to protect the lavish guardhouse while the off-duty guards feast, drink Dom Perignon, and play billiards inside.

This water pump, a functional replica of one located in the Yard in the 18th and 19th centuries, was built in the early 1980s with money given to the college by a wealthy alum specifically for "the construction of something quaint and/or picturesque, but not too expensive." The pump has been the Yard's only water source since 1985, when the 10-year-old winner of a "Harvard President for a Day " contest issued an irreversible order that all the Yard's water faucets be rigged to flow Orange Shasta.

Harvard's Science Center was built with funds donated by the Polaroid Corporation and is said to have been designed to look like a giant camera. In fact, on the day when the completed Center was opened to the public, nobody could figure out how to enter the building, and an angry crowd milled around outside for hours until someone finally realized that the architect had left the lens cap on. In 1987, Harvard made the building more accessible by removing it from its giant tripod and placing it on the ground. This picture of a camera was taken using the Science Center and a flash.

This is Emerson Hall, named after Ralph "Waldo" Emerson, and home of Harvard's philosophy department. One of the early scenes from the tearjerker movie *Love Story* was filmed here. The movie tells the story of a Radcliffe girl who, despite being married to a Harvard man, gets terminal cancer and dies. Emerson Hall's asbestos insulation was finally removed in 1987.

The Carpenter Center for the Visual Arts was built by a local street artist using only chalk, string, an open bit of sidewalk, and two million tons of reinforced concrete.

Memorial Hall, built in 1924,
commemorates those Harvard students
who made the ultimate sacrifice for their
country in World War I, volunteering
many of their best servants into the
army to fight and die overseas.
Memorial Hall contains a cavernous,
dark lecture hall named Sanders
Theater and an equally large and
somber rectangular hall used for exams.
The interior is so gloomy that halfway
through a 1989 concert in Sanders
Theater, singer Bobby "Don't Worry, Be
Happy" McFerrin suddenly walked off-
stage and hid in his dressing room, too
depressed to continue.

The Harvard Lampoon's ornate "Castle" was built in 1909 with money donated by publishing magnate and Lampoon alum William Randolph Hearst. That's us sitting on the front steps and taking a break from writing this book. *Our first free minute in 38 grueling months.*

Some would say it's a mistake to let you see that the gorilla is just a derelict who agreed to wear a costume in exchange for some food, but we think it adds a nice "behind-the-scenes" touch.

This concludes your photo tour. Once again, we welcome you to wondrous Harvard Yard. *Now git!*

A HISTORY OF HARVARD, BUT EXCITING

PRE-HISTORY: A DETAILED DESCRIPTION

Harvard College was begun in 1636 by the Great and General Court of the Massachusetts Bay Colony, which one day simply placed a brick on the ground, pointed at it, and said, "Harvard!" However, these quiet beginnings belie the hotly debated question of the new university's name, and for the longest time, voting was split among "Harvard," "Yale," "The United States of America," and "Ed Horkle."

THE EARLY, STUPID DAYS

For its first hundred years, Prestigious Harvard University was a relatively small college, and as a result its students were forced to stoop, shuffle, and hunch over. Eventually, Prestigious, Cramped Harvard began to grow larger, and its students kept pace, becoming tall, fat, and old. Professors evolved too, little by little shedding the matted hair and fierce mandibles of the mountain gorilla for the more placid accoutrements of the forest ape.

"THE CIVIL WAR" PLAYS HARVARD

Then another hundred years flew by and the Civil War began. Brother fought against brother, prompting America's preachers to give a series of love-one-another sermons in which they prayed fervently for more incest. As things escalated, however, the problem only mushroomed. Each family turned viciously against its own members: Father fought Father and Mother fought Mother. The dog continued to chase its own tail, as always, but now it was playing for keeps.

Equally epoch-making events were simultaneously transpiring

back at Harvard, which was embroiled in a heated controversy over which professor would get the best parking space.

WOMEN'S EDUCATION GETS SERIOUS

Somewhere along in here Harvard gained a companion university for women called Radcliffe College. This was in response to the long-observed fact that women needed a place to learn, as they were continually thumping men on the head and saying, "Us womens a'needs one 'a them schools." But Radcliffe was made a completely separate university from Harvard. Harvard and Radcliffe students used different libraries, dormitories, and classrooms, and rarely even ran into each other except in Harvard's Graduate School of Kissing.

THE ROARING TWENTIES

For Harvard students the Twenties was a time of fast partying, short haircuts, "flappers," and reading F. Scott Fitzgerald to see what the hell the other stuff was that they were supposed to be doing.

THE FIFTIES

The Fonz and Elvis. 'Nuff said.

THE SIXTIES

The Sixties was truly a difficult time of choices for Harvard students, because it was in this period that they were called on by their country to decide the fate of the Vietnam War. As always, youth saw the political situation for what it was—uninteresting, unless their own asses were on the line. There was, however, one heady day on which Harvard students boarded docked Coast Guard ships and tie-dyed Boston Harbor. It should be noted that anti-war protesters had no way of knowing that Asians whose lives were saved by ending the war would, twenty years later, fill up America's best colleges, causing the protesters' children to get rejected and have to attend Podunk U.

THE SEVENTIES

The Seventies, defined as those years when you watched Lee Majors successfully jump a moving dumptruck all because he had the "technology," found Harvard students *driving* that dumptruck. Graduates were tossed headlong into a more diverse, competitive job pool, in which having a Harvard diploma was no longer an assurance of finding work. Thus, the academic atmosphere at Harvard changed, becoming more aggressive and inquisitive: "Are you going to write me a good graduate school recommendation, Professor Whipple, or must I release the Kraken?"

HARVARD + RADCLIFFE = HARELIP

Also in the Seventies, Radcliffe finally merged with Harvard, and Harvard went all out for the ceremony. Dress was formal, Puritan-style. Boys wore big hats with buckles on them, knee-high black socks with the black pants that kind of cinch in above the socks, and carried blunderbusses; girls sported simple frocks, wore those napkins on their heads, and smoked the peace pipe.

The food tasted delicious. They catered it and there was lots of champagne and caviar, and these little sugar cookies dipped in chocolate sprinkles and flavoring and topped with a Hershey's peanut. Then, there were guys dressed like the different Norse heroes who walked around brandishing staffs and refilling your glass out of big goblets. Odin was this really nice black guy.

After people had milled around for a while, President Bok waved for silence, and everyone got real quiet. Then, this gigantic birthday cake was wheeled out, and a twelve-foot-tall naked girl, with the Radcliffe Constitution stamped in red on her forehead, popped out of it. She said, "Ta-da!" while the watching crowd of students, deans, dignitaries, and all the Kennedys, including Arnold, hooted and cheered and laughed.

THE EIGHTIES

In 1985, Harvard had its 350th anniversary celebration, very quietly, with the minimum of pomp and show, and just a few small, quiet, little fireworks which went off with a tiny "peep."

U.S. PRESIDENTS FROM HARVARD,
IN THEIR COLLEGE YEARS

- Theodore Roosevelt: A bandy-legged roustabout. Fond of sport, sweet-meat, and fancy-jacks.
- FDR: Around campus, the rakish young cripple was known as a coltish roustabout with a freakishly huge and dandified upper body.
- John Adams: Jackanape, rapscallion, and dirt-poor dock-walloper, he lux-uriated in brass baubles and lavish iron fripperies.
- John Q. Adams: Precisely the image of his indigent namesake. Partial to all manner of frippery and cavorting. A gen-u-ine shithead.
- JFK: A gallivanting rogue, he defined the height of rip-snorting, surlish waggery.
- Rutherford B. Hayes: Teetotaler, a real bore. But a flippant, dandyish scalawag nonetheless.

TIMELINE OF CRUCIAL EVENTS
IN HARVARD'S HISTORY

THEN   NOW

God shouts, "Alac-azam!" and a pointy-eared, bushy-tailed carrot-farmer named John Harvard hops onto the scene.

The admissions re-quirements are changed to include being smart as a criterion.

JFK graduates Harvard *magna cum laude*. Lee Harvey Oswald graduates *cum laude*, and Jack Ruby graduates without honors, set-ting off a vicious chain of jealousy and revenge.

Memorial Church is built underground out of mud and rocks. The univer-sity takes it on faith from the architect that it was ever ac-tually built.

Harvard fully opens its ivy-crowned gates to the common man; the rest of America becomes rich, arro-gant snots.

Fearless Freep dives off the highest spire of Memorial Hall, and into the out-stretched hands of "Moses," a local street beggar.

HARVARD TRADITIONS

Harvard is unique in that, since it's so old, student life is absolutely chock full of traditions. The administration considers this a great selling point and goes to great expense every year to discontinue old traditions and institute new ones, keeping them fresh and well-suited to ever-changing student tastes. A sampling . . .

SEX IN WIDENER LIBRARY

Harvard's Widener Library, named for an alumnus who asphyxiated in his sensory-deprivation tank aboard the *Hindenburg*, is a place for more than just studying. Every undergraduate hopes to have sex in Widener's extensive open stacks at least once before graduating. But because of Harvard students' tendencies toward procrastination and unattractiveness, this only results in hundreds of cap-and-gown-wearing seniors frantically masturbating there on Commencement Day.

THE FRESHMAN FIFTEEN

This term refers to the annual phenomenon of students gaining an average of 15 pounds during their first year at college. Remember, however, that 15 pounds only represents an *average* weight gain: for every freshman who adds 265 pounds, there is another who loses 250.

BUTTER-TOSSING IN THE FRESHMAN UNION

Walk into Harvard's huge, vaulted freshman dining hall and you'll see antique tables, antique portraits, antique tiling, and antique food—but that's not all. Each freshman class helps redecorate the hall by flinging pats of butter over 50 feet in the air, adhering them to the ceiling. Then, when alumni return to the Union for their fiftieth reunion dinner, their own individual pats of butter melt and gently drip down upon their heads, mingling with their tears of joy.

THE TRADITION OF "SIGNIFICANCE"

One of the oldest traditions at Harvard is the way every action and event on campus inevitably ends up having major global repercussions: A junior decides to change her concentration from Spanish Language and Civilization to Film Studies. Three days later, El Salvador, Guatemala, and Nicaragua are in political chaos. Three weeks later, there's a made-for-TV movie about it.

A sophomore submits a Government 1 paper which almost instantaneously leads to the dismantling of the Berlin Wall. (The paper was only given a B—had it received an A, a mile-deep trench would have been dug where the Wall had stood.)

A young child visits Harvard with his family. While walking through Harvard Yard he spies two ants. He steps on one, killing it. The other escapes. That ant becomes the President of Purdue University and an important member of Congress.

THE PRIMAL SCREAM

Harvard's campus typically resounds with high-pitched wails of varied origin, from students undergoing electroshock therapy to those simply afflicted with lycanthropy. But at midnight on the night before exams start, students traditionally open their windows and relieve their stress by loosing a great blood-curdling shriek known as the Primal Scream. This wakes up the students' Cambridge neighbors, who then traditionally come over and give them a good old-fashioned Primal Ass-Kicking.

APPLAUSE IN LECTURES

When a professor has finished lecturing to a large class, it is a Harvard tradition for the students to applaud. Sure, they've all heard him on tape, but the thrill of actually *being* there makes it sound so much better! Each student claps as loud as he can, hoping that his hoot, cheer, or wolf whistle will catch the professor's attention and win him an A. The last lecture in any course is a sight not to be missed. There is a standing ovation as the professor walks out of the room. Then the lighters come out, and the floor shakes with all the foot-stomping. Then finally, just when you thought it was over, the professor breaks through the chalkboard and the crowd screams for an encore—20 more minutes of lecture!

THE GAME: A HARVARD MEGATRADITION

The average Harvard football game is very poorly attended; it's always a hard struggle just to get the opposing team interested enough to show up. Once a year, however, the whole campus erupts with mild curiosity over the matchup against Ivy League archrival Yale, a contest so epochal that it is known simply as "The Game," or, more recently, "The Rolaids/American Express Game." Thousands of Harvard alumni fly back to Cambridge from all over the world to wave banners, blow airhorns, and cheer for their Alma Mater until they're hoarse, while watching the game on TV in the privacy of their lavish hotel rooms.

This leaves more room in the stadium for the students, who come in droves because there's always a rumor that someone famous will be there (Scott Baio or Tony Danza, depending on the year). Some students pull incredibly zany stunts at The Game, namely putting a dab of easily washed-off paint on their faces or wearing a few thick layers of clothing instead of many thin layers—even though it is often quite chilly! Most students, however, simply drink cheap, light brown vodka until they pass out, occasionally glancing at the scoreboard to see how much longer until the game is over and they can stop acting so goddamn collegiate.

Not that what happens on the field itself is always mind-numbingly boring. In fact, Harvard-Yale gridiron matchups (football games) have been the scene of some of the greatest sports comebacks ever: "You not only resent that remark, you resemble it!" (1908); "You *never*? Well then maybe you *should*!" (1945); and "Yeah? Well at least I'm not *you*!" (1969) are just a few of the now-classic snappy retorts first made by players during The Game.

When the Crimson and the Blue go head to head this fall, who will eat the Victory Stew?

Additionally, sometimes these football games contain some truly exceptional feats of athleticism. Just last year there was this beautiful play in which a Harvard guy just, well, you know, he just kind of . . . I mean the way this guy *just reached out and caught the darn ball*—well, take our word for it, it was really something! The Game is also exciting to watch because so much hangs in the balance, as its result determines which of the schools gets to call itself "Harvard" for the next year.

Some Traditional Harvard-Yale Game Cheers

Fight Song

Fightin' you, yeah, we're fightin' you.
Yeah, don't you know we're fightin'
you.
O Baby, don't you know we're
fightin' you.
Whole lotta fightin' goin' on.

Long Cheer

People say our cheers are lame,
But the other team is really lame.
We are going to win this game,
Because we are the better team in
this game.

Chorus:
You can fight us, it won't matter,
Unless you fight real hard, or with guns.
Then you might win and feel really glad,
But next year we'll be twice as mad.

No guns, please no guns!
Do not shoot us with your guns!

Our team will beat your team.
God will smile upon our victory.
Team.
Our skill and stalwart manner
Make us debonair. Manner.

Chorus:
The Brave Man dies a thousand deaths.
Let him—with only one funeral it's a
bargain.
Violence never solved anything except a
fight,
And might doesn't make right—which
rhymes with "fight."

Give us the ball.
And go get yourselves some therapy!

Short Cheer

Rah!

THE COMPUTER LITERACY/SWIM TEST

Every freshman is subjected to a variety of bizarre initiation rituals upon entering Harvard. The most grueling of these are the mandatory academic placement tests.

The very worst of these tests is the dreaded Computer Literacy/Swim Test. Most colleges require freshmen to take one or both of these tests, but, as always, Harvard expects a bit more of its students: They must take both tests *simultaneously.* To pass, one must swim one length of an Olympic-sized pool underwater, access the Harvard Mainframe Computer, answer a few questions, and swim back. Each student is allowed two breaths of air, and exam proctors circle constantly to watch for cheaters. The exam may take no longer than 30 minutes.

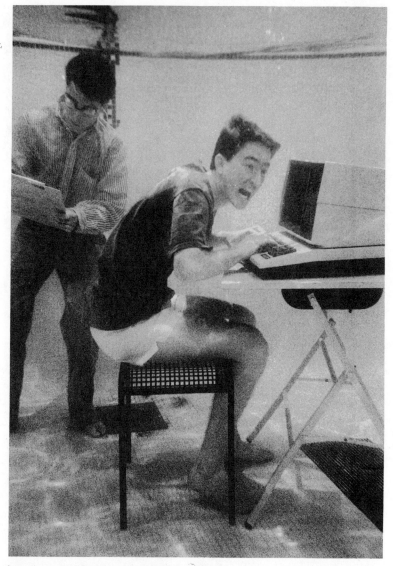

An exam proctor looks on as a student checks his answers during the final minutes of the Computer Literacy/Swim Test. The excitement of accessing Harvard's mainframe computer has left him breathless.

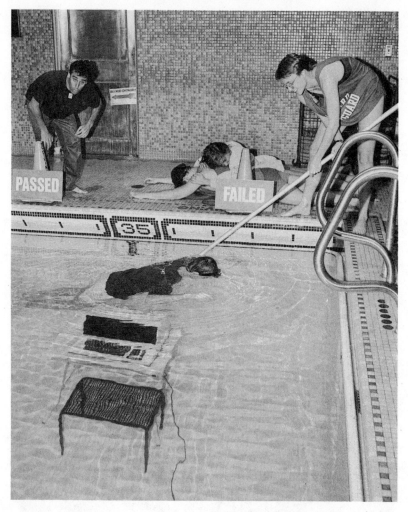

At the end of the exam, some students discuss how well they did.

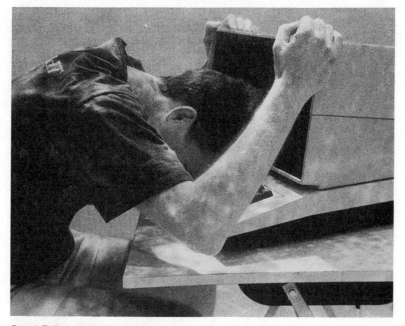

Dang! Failed *again*.

A PANTHEON OF FAMOUS HARVARD GRADUATES

As a reader of this book, you'll be joining the company of many of the people responsible for making the history of this country so boring. Harvard grads have done it all. They've made peace between nations, cured scourging plagues, sent a dog to Venus—a few even wrote this book. The following are some of Harvard's greatest heroes:

Cotton Mather, a 17th-century man of God, set forth extremely rigorous academic guidelines for himself while at Harvard, guidelines which he knew would be impossible to maintain. A firm believer in strict discipline, Mather was able to convince his instructors to give him incredibly high marks, marks which he would bear on his body for the rest of his life.

Nineteenth-century philosopher **Ralph Waldo Emerson** is renowned for his theory of Transcendentalism, which states that the most intimate part of yourself is that which you share in common with all of Mankind. To prove his point, Emerson would often stand in the middle of Harvard Yard and offer his dirty underwear to passersby, forcing the vile rags upon the few Non-Transcendentalists who dared refuse them.

Publishing mogul **William Randolph Hearst** was expelled from Harvard for repeatedly disrupting on-campus showings of the film *Citizen Kane*, shouting, "That's a lie!" during parts which he felt inaccurately represented what his life would be like.

One of the most enigmatic of Harvard's alumni is **Henry Kissinger.** As an undergraduate, Kissinger spent a great deal of his time becoming famous. He became involved in student government and quickly created and filled the position of Student Council Emperor. While holding this post, Kissinger first tested many of the theories of international diplomacy which would later gain him notoriety, dropping water balloons on the heads of passing Vietnamese exchange students from his fifth-floor dormroom window and, in order to reopen Harvard undergraduate ties with China, making numerous trips to visit Chairman Mao Tse-Tung (then a comely coed at Wellesley).

John Fitzgerald Kennedy learned at an early age that he had polio and was Irish. But, never one to be beaten by adversity, in college he designed a grueling physical therapy program which involved having sex with every woman on earth. In 1942, during his senior year, he heard there were 109 women in France willing to have sex with him, and set sail for Europe immediately, christening his yacht the *Poon Tang 109*. When German sailors who were dat-

ing the women interposed themselves, the lust-crazed Kennedy
leaped upon their boat, puncturing
and sinking it.

Fred Grandy, who once played
"Gofer" on the hit TV series "Love
Boat," is now a U.S. Representative
whose political star is rising, excit-
ing, and new, on Washington's hori-
zon. Welcome aboard the Ship of
State, Fred, we're expecting you.
Fred's platform promises something
for everyone, and he'll be making another run in 1992, this time for the
office of Senator—life's sweetest re-
ward. And since Fred claims bald
men inspire him with loyalty, he may
have his sights set on an eventual VP
slot in a Presidential ticket with either John Glenn or Telly Savalas.

That's right, *Gofer* went to Harvard.

A WORD FROM YOUR PROFESSORS

"Ahem. Harrumph harrumph harrumph harrumph harrumph harrumph harrumph. Ahem. Snort. (Pounding podium.) Harrumph harrumph harrumph harrumph harrumph harrumph harrumph harrumph harrumph harrumph harrumph. Mumble mumble. (Stroking chin.) Sniff. Harrumph harrumph. Grunt. Mutter. Harrumph. Eh? No. Harrumph harrumph harrumph harrumph harrumph harrumph harrumph harrumph harrumph harrumph harrumph harrumph. (Pointing finger.) Mutter. Snort. Sniff. Harrumph harrumph harrumph harrumph harrumph harrumph harrumph harrumph harrumph harrumph harrumph. Grunt grunt. Sniff. Ahem. Snort. Mutter. Harrumph. You take the point."

Not *all* professors are like this. Only the truly *great* ones.

BASIC TRAINING

STUDY SKILLS

This book won't do anything for you unless you read it the way a Harvard student would—that is, in an English translation of the original French. The Harvard student also has a veritable Batman's utility belt full of study skills that make life a little easier. We suggest you follow these tips, lest this book's wisdom fall through your head and make a mess all over the new throw rug.

- The first thing you ought to do is **create a study environment**, one with the proper atmosphere for the completion of your task. Buy a case of your favorite malt liquor, drink it in front of the television, and pass out while watching MTV's "Tattoo Cher's Butt" Contest. When you wake up, replace your reading lamp with a strobe light and your desk with a disco ball. Now you are ready to begin.
- But before you do, you must create a **work schedule** for yourself. A schedule is a good motivating tool, and you'll be needing motivation, what with your study environment. Get your calendar out and set dates for the completion of each chapter and also a final date by which you will have finished the entire book. Now, do nothing but read comic books and fantasize until that date. Okay, you're back. God, you'd *really* better get to work.
- At this point, you'll never finish on time if you can't **speed read.** Here's a simple exercise to help you along: Read this sentence. Read this one faster. Read this one faster. Read this one faster read this one faster *read this one faster read this one faster read this one faster.* You hear that bang? *You've just broken the sound barrier, my friend!*
- To get the most out of this book, you have to **take notes** as you read. A Harvard student takes notes by highlighting every sentence in the book with a fluorescent yellow marker, copying all highlighted material into a spiral notebook, losing both the book and the notebook, and photocopying someone else's notes the night before the test.
- Notes are useless if you're not **organized.** For this, we strongly suggest

43

purchasing a Mead Trapper-Keeper®. This wonderful item is no conventional three-ring binder. The rings slide rather than "clip" together, and it contains a bunch of pockets and folders for your papers. Best of all, it all closes neatly and safely with a Velcro strip. And if you can't pass the Trapper-Keeper® through your entire digestive tract without smudging a single page, you get your money back.

THE ALL-NIGHTER

The Harvard undergraduate's unofficial motto is, "Never put off till tomorrow what you can do in the throes of amphetamine psychosis the last night before it's due." Now that is your motto, too. College students everywhere pull all-nighters, but at Harvard, students are not only smarter and richer than elsewhere, but also much, much lazier. You're staying up all night? You've got lots of time. It'd be a shame to waste all that time studying. There's a Dick van Dyke retrospective on, you know . . .

CHEATING

There's a famous story at Harvard about a student who was suspected of cheating. His only defense was that he had gotten his answers from God! Well, the disciplinary board checked the files, and apparently God *had* taken the course the year before. Their tests had the same answers—a miracle! Harvard kicked them both out.

As you can see, Harvard takes cheating very seriously, and so do Harvard students. Here are some of the ways students have managed to spend their book money on weekend trips to Aspen and still score straight A's.

METHOD 1: Writing on the Hand

The Fake Watch-Check.

The Checking-the-Fingernails Gambit.

The Señor Wences Maneuver.

METHOD 2: Plagiarism

Students will try to get away with anything when it comes to plagiarism. A guy writing a history paper on the Civil War turned in the Gettysburg Address, and for an architectural drawing class someone signed her name to a postcard of the Colosseum in Rome.

METHOD 3: Morse Code

Chief among the conspiracy-type cheat methods is the use of Morse code. While in the exam room, friends will often signal answers to thorny questions with alternating long and short coughs, belches, yawns, noseblows, fingersnaps, or whatever. Some particularly difficult exams have sounded like a tropical forest in wildebeest mating season.

The danger is that those caught cheating with Morse are forced to enlist in the Navy and help land F-16s on aircraft carriers for the rest of their lives. Therefore, students typically prefer to silently wink their illicit, coded information. Even this is risky, however, as many lust-crazed exam proctors may mistake a misdirected wink for a come-on and leap upon the cheater, sexing him to death before his pen hits the floor.

METHOD 4: The Bathroom Gambit

The bathroom has always been an easy place to cheat and a convenient place to relieve oneself. Crib sheets are often kept in the bathroom taped to one of the stalls. Unfortunately, a few of the more muscular exam proctors often stake out the bathroom and give suspected cheaters swirlies until exam time has elapsed. Also, some campus men's rooms are notorious as sites for anonymous homosexual activities. Thus, a little mix-up could provide a student with answers to the anatomy exam he never dreamed of taking.

METHOD 5: Cheat Sheets

Answers. The teacher wants to see them in writing. So do you. At the beginning of every exam, the proctors will tell you to put all your bags, books, papers, and computers off to one side, but the wily student will disguise his cheat sheet as a putt-putt score card or a list of emergency phone numbers. The craftiest students write information on Kleenex or handkerchiefs, hence the phrase "divining snot," heard often around exam time.

The big problem with this kind of cheating is what info to cram onto your small card. Tricky vocab words are best for language tests; dates are good for history exams; for multiple-choice tests, random letters will do.

METHOD 6: Sicking Out

Another ever-popular cheating method is the sick-out. There are several ways to try to sick out, some

successful, some not, all involving a painful meeting with a nurse at University Health Services. Let's observe:

[*Student enters, obviously not sick.*]

STUDENT: I'm sick. Boy am I sick. I'm so sick I can't take my exam.

NURSE: But you don't look sick.

(*Student sneezes, then sneezes again a little louder. Looks at nurse questioningly*)

N: You are not sick.

S: (*coughs a little*) How's that?

M: Not sick.

S: How about if I wear a sombrero, stand outside the Student Union and chafe my buttocks with a hedge clipper while crooning "Under the Boardwalk" to passersby?

N: You're sick!

S: Great! Can I have my medical excuse?

METHOD 7: Artificial Intelligence

You can always just give up and have someone else take your exams, but this method is far from foolproof: Ted Kennedy, '65, was expelled because he picked the wrong person to take an exam for him. The professor, far from flattered by the offer, was so angry that he gave Teddy a D−.

Consequently, many of the brightest students try to eliminate the human element by building a cyborg likeness of themselves out of answering machines, beer cans, and wallet-sized yearbook photos. These machines are preprogrammed with all the material covered in the course plus a few juicy articles on the subject from *Reader's Digest*. The biggest difficulty is that many of the machines aren't user-friendly, and many students have been caught when their cyborg completed the test, handed it in, and then kicked the exam proctor in the testicles.

METHOD 8: Telepathy

Those students blessed with psychic powers can freely scan the minds of the smartest, best-prepared students in any class, both for exam questions and for term-paper ideas. Yet rarely does a professor adjust these students' grades, taking their gifts into account, as he knows he may be psychically induced to lose control of his bowels at his next tenure review meeting.

HARVARD DRINKING GAMES

You might be surprised to see "drinking games" discussed here in the "Basic Training" section. "Drinkin' games," you sneer, "that's one thing you Harvard types can't tell me an' my buddies jack shit about. Maybe we should sit down an' write a big ol' book about drinkin' games, an' teach you eggheads a thing 'r two!" Well, these are special drinking games, Harvard style. Go ahead and play them without worrying a jot about disrupting your studies.

π**(Pi):** Players take turns reciting the digits of π *after* 3.14159265. No one makes a mistake, so no one has to drink.

I never: Players sit in a circle and take turns admitting things they never did, like having sex or drinking a beer. Other players shake their heads and say, "Gosh, me neither," or, "Gee whiz, I wonder what it's like."

Questions: Players gather in groups by major and ask each other study questions. If someone doesn't know the answer to a question, he must change majors and think seriously about his future at Harvard. This is no time to get drunk.

Supply & Demand: Players suppose that x kegs of beer were to be purchased for y guests, and then estimate per capita consumption curves and predict the time the hypothetical party would end. When that time arrives, they go to bed.

Suicide Attempt: For one player. Player writes a long note complaining about academic stress, grabs a bottle of bourbon and a handful of sleeping pills, realizes he doesn't drink or do drugs, and instead eats a quart of ice cream.

Computer-Animated Quarters: Players use the J, K, and L keys (or joystick) to bounce a high-resolution quarter into the cup, taking into account computer-generated air currents and tabletop elasticity. When a player misses, the computer becomes less responsive to his inputs, in a remarkable simulation of the sluggishness caused by excessive drinking.

A pair of Harvard men enjoying the traditional Harvard drink, an *extra*-dry Martini. To prepare: hold a Martini glass to your mouth and just whisper the word "Vermouth." Then whisper the word "gin." Enjoy!

Part
III

LET'S LEARN TOGETHER!

HEY, WHY DON'T YOU TEACH US SOME *REAL* STUFF?

You must have read our mind. Now that you've settled in at Harvard and mastered the basic abilities necessary to see you through a Harvard education, we can begin your coursework. A few things are worth noting here, before we send you rollerblading down the hallowed halls of academia:

A. EXTRACURRICULARS

No college student studies *all* the time, not even at Harvard. The student has to find a way to refresh the mind and let off steam. But Harvard students are known for their deep and serious involvement in extracurricular activities, some of which are even more demanding in time and energy than their studies.

For you, this translates into playing a hard game of Super Mario Bros. every few pages, or perhaps pausing between chapters to break up some Gaines-Burgers for the dog's dinner.

B. STUDENT-FACULTY INTERACTION

Besides extracurriculars, another thing you'd be doing if you were *really* going to Harvard is attending the occasional lecture. Harvard prides itself on its unusually accomplished faculty, and Harvard students enjoy personal interaction with these academic superstars on a daily basis. We can't claim to be giving you a complete Harvard education unless we provide something similar. This situation calls for some role-playing, as follows:

(1) Get yourself a pair of Groucho glasses—the kind with the nose and mustache attached.

(2) Set aside an hour or two when you can be alone without interruptions. Listen to some quiet music, take a hot bath, have a cup of your favorite herbal tea or a glass of wine—do whatever you usually do to unwind. When you feel fully relaxed, stand in front of the mirror and don the disguise.

(3) *Now you're The Professor.* Dignified, eloquent, intimidatingly brilliant. Explore your new identity—probe your new mind and body—and act out your most secret fantasies.

(4) Remove the disguise.

(5) Now you're you again, meek and cowed in the awesome presence of The Professor.

(6) Enjoy dialogues between your two identities. Watch them share, develop, and define themselves in terms of each other. Become confident and smooth in your transitions. For example:

You: Um, excuse me ... Professor?

The Professor: GAAAAH! Once again, you've interrupted my train of thought! What manner of foolishness is it *this* time, *pray tell*?

You: Oh, well, I'm having some trouble with Proust, and I—

The Professor: IDIOT!!! FETCH ME MY HICKORY ROD, AND DON'T TARRY!

You: yessiryessiryessiryessir

Now, take the next big step:

(7) *Go out into public as The Professor.*

The first time, you'll only stroll through the park or go to the movies. But by the second or third time you'll find yourself making small talk at a bar or stepping out to a dance club. And soon the day will come when you, as The Professor, invite your first starry-eyed "student" up to the luxurious apartment you've taken across town from your home ...

C. CHOOSING YOUR FIELD OF STUDY

Finally, before you start studying, you have to figure out *what* to study. If you tried to study everything, something precious in your head would break, and you'd end up on the street corner selling mugs filled with pencils to blind guys.

We understand that this can be a difficult decision to make: When so few subjects interest you, how can you commit to *one* with any confidence? To help you out, we provide the following fashion-magazine-style quiz. Just do what the questions say, and the quiz will do all the thinking for you.

☐ Anthropology, 57
☐ Biology, 68
☐ Classics, 76
☐ Computer Science, 77
☐ Economics, 84
☐ English, 91
☐ Fine Arts, 99
☐ Folklore and Mythology, 107
☐ Foreign Languages and Cultures, 112
☐ Government, 119
☐ Hard Sciences, 122
☐ History, 130
☐ Linguistics, 133
☐ Mathematics, 138
☐ Philosophy, 144
☐ Psychology, 150
☐ Religion, 156
☐ Visual and Environmental Studies, 164

1) How many glaring, unforgivable inaccuracies did you notice in the movie *Quest For Fire*? Put that many checks next to Anthropology.

2) Do you reproduce asexually? If so, have each of your clones put a check next to Biology.

3) On a scale of one to ten, rate the following joke: "*The Odyssey* is about 'Odysseus.' *The Iliad* is about 'Iliadeus.'" Put that many checks next to Classics.

4) How many roses did you buy for your Commodore Vic-20 last Valentine's Day? Put that many checks next to Computer Science.

5) What percent interest did you charge your father on his second mortgage? Put that many checks next to Economics.

6) How many of Shakespeare's plays were actually written by *you*? Put that number of checks by English.

7) Put a check by Fine Arts for each time you are mentioned in Andy Warhol's diary.

8) How many pet stores have you visited trying to find a griffin? Put that number of checks next to Folklore and Mythology.

9) How many times are you willing to swing at a *piñata* before giving up? Put that many checks next to Foreign Languages and Cultures.

10) How many times did you vote for yourself in the last Presidential election? Put that many checks by Government.

11) How many of your kids are named after noble gases? Put that many checks by Hard Sciences.

12) Put a check next to History for every time you have bored your grandparents with tales of the "good ol' days."

13) How many seconds do you wait before finishing a stutterer's sentence? Put that many checks next to Linguistics.

14) How many of the integers do you have nicknames for? Put that many checks by Mathematics.

15) How many beads of blood appear on your forehead when someone answers "because" after you ask "why"? Put that many checks next to Philosophy.

16) Pull down your pants and count up all the phallic symbols you observe. Put that many checks next to Psychology.

17) Put a check by Religion for every time you have been to synagogue in the last year.

18) Put a check by Visual and Environmental Studies for every letter you wrote to Ted Turner expressing your outrage at his colorization of *Abbott and Costello Meet the Mummy*.

That's the quiz. Now count it up and score it, just as you would in *Cosmo*:

- **80–100 checks:** Well, hello, hot stuff!!! You certainly don't seem to have any problem getting exactly what you want from a relationship. But be careful; someone as dynamic as you are can sometimes appear obnoxious.

- **60–80 checks:** You may not actually be bulimic, but you should ease off on your risky habits. Don't be afraid to talk to your physician or a dietary counselor about anything that's concerning you.

- **40–60 checks:** You really don't know very much at all about Vanilla Ice. But it's never too late!

- **0–40 checks:** You're hopeless. You're pathetic. You're disgusting. Your major is the one with the most checks by it, so turn to the appropriate page and get crackin'. But do that later—right now, report directly to your beautician for a thorough rethinking of your make-up strategy.

ANTHROPOLOGY

Anthropology is the study of Man, and Harvard's department is one of the world's best, as many Men have worked there over Harvard's three and a half centuries.

Within the anthropology department itself one can find excellent case studies, from the long-necked geek who knows everything except how to avoid injury when using the photocopier, to the Malaysian cultures grad student who can't speak a word of English but can always trick the long-necked geek to run off some copies for him.

FRESHLY DUG-UP VOCABULARY WORDS

Reproductive physiology: What kind of shape you're in determines your chances at reproducing and seeing your genes carried into the next generation. As usual, shape means size and the bigger you are means the more you can mate, while the smaller male members of the species are resigned to sit around in groups making lewd comments about the females and hoping the big guys catch a foul disease.

Primate: What we are. And all apes and monkeys and lemurs and lorises and tarsiers, too. Feel gifted and special? You don't even know what those last 3 animals *look* like.

Hominoid: This classification contains the very first human-like animals. The word itself means, "those who aren't afraid to eat off the ground." All of the other species died out, except for the strain that finally led to the species of Man, and one other which became supervillains.

Hominid: Mankind's most recent ancestors: *Homo habilis*, so named because he was handy with tools, followed by *Homo erectus*, who outlived his cousin by learning the importance of keeping tools away from children.

And who were his children? *Homo sapiens* (that's us!) and *Homo neanderthalis*, who both lived side by side in peace and harmony until one day *Homo sapiens* split open Neanderthal's head with an axe. Just got tired of lookin' at the freak.

Behavioral ecology: What you want to eat determines the way you act. Careful studies have shown, for example, that when a primate wants food he tends to act hungry.

Adaptive mutation: When a genetic mutation actually improves an organism's chance of survival (or even just plain enjoyment in its environment). An everyday example:

"The radiation from the plutonium buried on Mrs. Johnson's property caused her three children to mutate so that they are perfectly adapted to their backyard. 'Seven hands are better than two for climbing my favorite tree!' says Frankie. Meanwhile, the horn on Susie's head helps her to catch fireflies, and little Johnny Jr.'s tail helps him to float quickly downstream.'"

HARVARD MAN

COURSES

ANTHROPOLOGY 110: Biological Anthropology

Biological anthropology is an academic centaur—part hard-core science, part horse. The bio anthro concentrator must constantly deal with many perplexing questions, the most common of which is, "What is bio anthro?" or, "What is biological anthropology?" or, "What is biological anthro?" or, "What is *that*?" Such questions, like many others the concentrator must face, can only be asked during conversation with other people. Thus, the concentrator quickly learns to hide alone in his lab and never answer the phone.

But bio anthro does arm the student with an armada of terms from its special lexicon. The department line is that bio anthro specializes in nutritional ecology, human reproductive physiology, and biological paleontology and paleohistology. The result is that absolutely no one knows what they're doing or why they're here, and a lion's share of inexpensive beer is consumed.

Bio anthro is an area of study rife with contradictions. It is a discipline that studies monkeys to understand Man, which is kind of like asking the guy who pumps your gas what kind of underwear the CEO of Exxon likes. Students in bio anthro must take courses on people so old that they're dead. On people so dead that they're fossilized. Taught by people so fossilized that they can only be tenured professors.

They also must enjoy a course on sex in which they learn that if humans were capable of asexual reproduction, then every time someone masturbated they'd have a baby. And a course on human biology in which they learn that if the Exxon CEO has any brains he'll wear boxers so he doesn't fry his sperm in a pair of lime green banana-hammocks.

ANTHROPOLOGY 113: Social Anthropology

Social anthropology is the study of foreign cultures by people who have failed to fit into their own. The idea is that by becoming interested in a society a long way away, the student can pretend to be "in" somewhere else and can scorn the society where he now lives and is far too insecure to leave.

The philosophy is simple: A person who builds mud lean-tos becomes interesting if he is doing it halfway around the world, preferably on the top of a mountain or in some other hellhole. (A person who constructs lean-tos on this side of the globe is called a *hobo*.)

ANTHROPOLOGY 117: Archaeology

Archaeology is considered the "pre-professional" wing of the anthropology department, as students graduate to fill a variety of custodial positions in Cambridge and beyond. One of the neat things archaeology students can do is play with stone tools, which is fun until someone awls himself in the eye.

As human societies evolved, there have always been derelicts and homeless scavengers who sifted through debris and unwanted refuse. Now society has advanced enough to give these people a whole science to do whatever they want.

Archaeology is based on strange principles. No one wanted this stuff 2,000 years ago, so you'd think we'd realize it's garbage by now. But, interestingly enough, if something no one wants hangs around long enough, it can, at the right time, become pretty valuable. Like the last fat girl at a frat party.

Archaeology professors have created special, gimmicky methods to try to "liven" up the "dead" material of their discipline. One of the most popular methods is that of "role-playing," in which the student tries to gain insight into the lives of our distant ancestors by fantasizing that he is a prehistoric man. Even if the student does get arrested for murdering local dogs, he often contracts double pneumonia and dies.

ANTHROPOLOGY 134: Garbology

Garbology, the analysis of a culture's refuse to gain insights into that culture, has emerged as one of anthropology's most exciting new techniques.

Garbologists (or "junkies," as they are known if they are also drug addicts) hate to admit that this still ranks it as deathly boring in the general scheme of things. They are quick to point out that their field remains as much an art as a science, a ploy which enables them to win twice as many government grants as they legitimately deserve.

Here Dr. Franco Mungucherello has agreed to demonstrate how garbologists translate the "raw data" found in the field into incredibly detailed knowledge of past civilizations.

Location of Dig: Outside Haifa, Israel.

Dr. Mungucherello's analysis: "Let's see, what do we got here? Okay, a used condom over there, an old soup can, *another* used condom . . . Jeez, no *wonder* the Philistines died out!"

Location of Dig: Yucatán Peninsula, Mexico.

Dr. Mungucherello's analysis: "All right, we got some moldy banana peels, some, what is this, *fish*? Mother Mary, this stuff reeks to high heaven! Let's get out of here—all you need to know is those Mayans must have had one hell of a filthy, disgusting, smelly culture. Stink-*O*."

Location of Dig: Olduvai Gorge, Kenya.

Dr. Mungucherello's analysis: "This is just a bunch of old, old trash. I doubt that sifting through this crap would serve any purpose."

Location of Dig: Silanas, Greece.

Dr. Mungucherello's analysis: "It's clear that the ancient civilization which flourished here was just beginning to develop the concept of 'garbage' as we know it. I mean, they didn't just throw out junk, here. In fact, I bet my old lady could use some of this stuff in her apartment—Hey, Vinny, back up the truck!"

ANTHROPOLOGY 223: Man and His Tools

Tools are what separate Man from the animals. Though an antelope or muskrat can instinctively select the appropriate screwdriver, only a human can truly *know* which one is the Phillips. It's not surprising, then, that the story of Man's evolution from hunch-backed Neanderthal to hairy-backed guy who grosses everyone out at the beach is largely a story of tools. Indeed, anthropologists have divided the history of *Homo sapiens* into discrete periods corresponding to advances in the sophistication and style of the tools he used, as shown in the fossil records past societies have left behind.

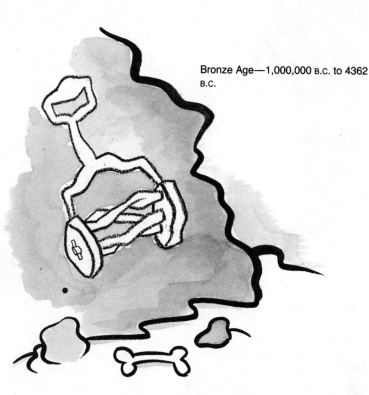

Bronze Age—1,000,000 B.C. to 4362 B.C.

Tools like this one, pictured in a cave painting dated to 600,000 B.C., indicate that at this time Man was beginning to take an interest in horticulture, and yet was still largely a hunter-gatherer in need of lightweight, mobile possessions. Iron smelting capabilities are still millennia away.

Silver Age—4362 B.C. to 1000 B.C.

Artifacts from this period show that Man was finally beginning to settle down in permanent dwellings and establish lifelong monogamous relationships. Rudimentary iron-smelting knowledge is hinted at, but there is no direct evidence of it.

Gold Age—1000 B.C. to 1812 A.D.

At this stage, Man had greatly improved his lot with the invention of the blade protector, automatic safety release, and push-button start-up. Iron smelting almost certainly began to be practiced toward the end of this period, although it was apparently still uncommon and done very crudely.

Space Age—1812 A.D. to 1949 A.D.

With the space age came a more sedentary, leisurely, and "deluxe" life-style. The trademark of the times were variable rotor speed, three gears, and snowplow-conversion capabilities. All iron-smelting technology was lost at some point during this period.

Man has now invented tools of such power that they threaten civilization's very existence. The picture on the following page does not depict reality—yet—but rather is meant to be a chilling warning of what Man may be reduced to if he does not start controlling the machines he himself created. To maintain our front lawns without the aid of tools—to have to graze for hours every Sunday morning—in the aftermath of a global apocalypse is a fate we can still avoid.

Post-Nuclear Age—1949 A.D. to ???

BIOLOGY

You might say that God was the first biologist—animals, plants, and such were His specialty. Modern biologists try to be like God in their own little ways, whether it's looking at germs, grinding up organs, or gulping down big buckets of "enzymes." Through these methods, they have managed to create some pretty decent animals of their own, such as the liger, the beefalo, and the biological warfare.

At Harvard, of course, biology majors have to start a little smaller than that. They can't just go in on their first lab day and create a million-foot redwood. The best a bio major can hope for freshman year is to make a cool-looking bug or some really slippery algae. With this understood, let us examine the subject matter of this most icky of the sciences.

THE TERMS OF WHICH LIFE ITSELF IS MADE

Symbiosis: When two kinds of animals have a relationship that benefits them both. The classic example of this is the rhino and the tiny dickie bird. The rhino teaches the dickie bird the craft of magic, and the dickie bird, in turn, agrees not to reveal the identity of his reclusive mentor.

Photosynthesis: The process by which plants use sunlight to create food. At night, they have to order out for pizza like everyone else.

Cell: The building block of life. A cell is to a person as a Lincoln log is to a mile-high wooden person.

Chromosome: This tiny particle, transmitted during sex, carries the genetic code used to build a new organism. A good thing, since it would be incredibly painful to pass microfilm through the average urethra.

Species: A group of animals that, when they mate together, produce fertile offspring. Though of different species, monkeys and pigs will continue to enjoy great sex together in defiance of scientists' Puritanical taboos.

Fear the day when genetic engineering sends this clockwork monstrosity lumbering through your carrot patch.

COURSES

BIOLOGY 1: Introduction to Biology

The secret to biology is that there are only a few basic animals. All other animals are just combinations of these four:

COW

FISH

OKAPI

RAT

Let's try a few examples:

Lizard: One part fish, one part rat.

LIZARD

Seagull: Rats with wings.

SEAGULL

Platypus: Not actually an animal, unless the definition of the word is stretched to include "platypus."

Okapi: Self-explanatory.

Bear: Three parts cow, one part rat.

BEAR

Horse: Cow.

HORSE

BIOLOGY 110: Critter Facts

Much of biology consists of the collection and memorization-at-gunpoint of obscure facts about critters. When your gardener says, "Boy, it sure was hard work pulling up all these *weeds*," and walks up to you with your prize-winning orchids clutched in his hands, say, "Why, yooooouuu *idiot!*" and have him read this section.

• The rhinoceros's horn is actually made up of thousands of individual hairs, three bottles of Dep Super-Hold, and the styling magic of Mister ShaMarr.

- The Amazonian gabbo root, when mashed, dried, and eaten, recreates the physical sensation of puking up the Amazonian gabbo root.
- Cats eat mice and dogs eat cats and dog catchers eat dogs.
- Ostriches can fly, but they need a 2-mile running start, a cliff to jump from, zero gravity, rocket boosters, the body of a different kind of bird, and, above all, the *desire.*
- Porcupines cannot actually "shoot" their quills. *If they could, they would be far too powerful.*

- A red rose means "I love you"; a pink rose means "I like you"; a white rose means "We're friends"; a transparent rose means "I have no idea who you are."

- The "panda bear" isn't really a "bear"; in fact, it isn't really a "panda," either.
- It is now believed that the "mermaids" sighted by sailors over the centuries were really nothing but manatees. The manatee is a sea mammal with the lower body of a fish and the upper body of a beautiful naked woman.
- The opossum is well known for playing dead to get rid of predators. Dead opossums that play alive are even more successful at this.

BIOLOGY 145: The Mysteries of Sex

We wanted to do this right, so we got it straight from the sex-ridden mouth of noted Harvard sexologist Dr. Emile Orgasmo:

"As a Professor of Sexual Biology, I am appalled by the extent of sexual ignorance in our society. Few people

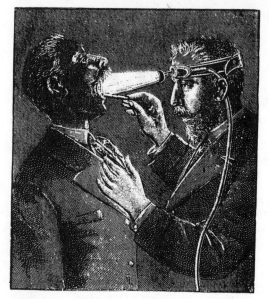

Dr. Orgasmo collects some "data."

know what a penis is. Even fewer have ever had an orgasm. And breasts! Most people can't even fathom them. Our minds are in the Space Age but our genitals are still with the dinosaurs. In our public schoolyards, many teenagers have more sex in five minutes than their parents have in a lifetime.

"Forget the birds and the bees. I'm going to be honest and direct about everything, and I mean *everything* you've ever wanted to know about sex but were afraid to ask . . ."

Where's the woman's G-spot?

"The woman's G-spot has not yet been located for certain. The man's G-spot, however, is definitely the vagina."

How big is the normal penis?

"Good question! How big is a man's hat? Big enough to fit his head. How many rolls of string does it take to go from the earth to the moon? One, if it's long enough. Get the point? A penis is as large as it needs to be so that it can reach what it has to reach."

Yes, but how big is the normal penis?

"The preoccupation with penis size has brought about many interesting rituals. Whenever two men meet in a public shower or YMCA locker room, their eyes immediately go to each other's penises. They then take out rulers and measure each other. The man with the larger penis receives accolades and his rival's black address book. The loser gets a dollar."

Is it true that the clitoris is simply a miniature penis? And if a man touches it, does that mean he's gay?
"Yes."

BIOLOGY 258: Animal Behavior

Why does an animal act the way he does? You might as well ask, Why does a human being act the way he does? Simple. Usually, he's horny. Thus we conclude our discussion of animal behavior.

Biologists get most of their information about animal behavior from the diaries of the animals themselves. Consider:

My Life as a Dog
by Rex

Today: Yawned twice. Sat. Licked myself in front of company. Barked.
Today: Sat. Slept. Watched tail. Slept. Watched tail until it went away. Ate box of crayons.
Today: Shat on carpet in 64 different colors. Slept. Climbed on furniture, soiling it with paws. Barked.
Today: Tail came back! Chased it all day.
Today: Ate. Shat. Ate shit. Threw up. Ate throw-up. Shat. Barked.

Today: Tail, tail, and more tail! A great day.
Today: Thought about licking myself, but no one else was at home. Shat.
Today: A tail extravaganza! Luckily found time to eat, sleep, bark.
Today: Ate some food from a new bowl. Watched Dad come in and flush bowl. Slept.
Today: Slept. Worried that there may be more to life. Musings interrupted by tail. Shat, then ate.

BIOLOGY 262: The Theory of Evolution

Most people like to think that Darwin was just the guy who thunk up "survival of the fittest." Far from it. Darwin not only originated the concept, he enforced it. If a bunch of little rabbits banded together to gang up on a big lion, Darwin would be there brandishing a machine gun and waving a scolding finger. He also did his part to help the food chain along. He would catch a fish, then feed the fish to a bigger fish, then feed the bigger fish to a killer whale, and so on until you got to Darwin, stuffing his face at a seafood restaurant.

The Evolution of Modern Man— from Dog to Cat and Back Again

Past Man:

In a time not so far distant, the world was a very tough place, and Man was just another protoplasmic

Past Man.

Future Man.

entity struggling to raise a family in it, while desperately trying to learn how sex worked. Then a tiny amoeba, our forefather, managed to advance far enough that it was just able to flop itself up onto land and evolve into Erik Estrada.

Sixty million years and the Tyrannosaurus Rex later, Man became a furry, warm-blooded rodent with a fire in his belly. He spent his days searching for a "New York City," where Chinese restaurants with open eggroll storage bins were rumored to abound.

Future Man:

Man the animal is continually adapting, increasing his survival capacity by building on his stronger traits and shedding his less useful ones, until that far-distant hour in the misty future, when he will be little more than a walking, talking, reasoning appendix.

In that final moment of epiphany, let us hope that there will be some changes. Before the lights blare; before the unseen forces of the cosmos whisk us up to join the millions of other fully evolved beings from every corner of the universe in an entity constructed from lattices of pure energy; before the sun explodes and becomes the size of a shoe insert; before all that stuff happens, perhaps people can just decide to love one another, and shit like that. We can but hope.

BIOLOGY 310: Human Anatomy, Specifically, the Appendix

The appendix is the most useless part of our bodies; it's always getting in everyone's way. If you trip and fall, it guarantees that there will be marbles, banana peels, and tines-up rakes in your path. If you knock your head against something, it fits the aspirin bottle with a child-proof cap.

If you forget someone's name, it ensures that he will be angry enough to pursue strict retaliatory measures like firing you from your job, or sending you insulting mail.

But wait, don't get it removed! Consider what happened to my friend Eugenio. Eugenio is in the hospital for routine stomach surgery, and as a preventative measure the doctor removes his appendix. Which is great. In no time he's fully recovered and goes home to relax with his family. Two days later, Eugenio contracts appendicitis. What then? Go back to the hospital, dig through the dumpsters, and have his appendix hastily reinstalled? Learn from Eugenio's example. You'll be advised to keep your appendix, and leave cosmetic surgery to the fashion-conscious.

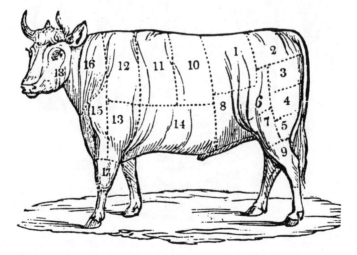

The first-year biology final exam includes an oral section in which the professor says a number and the student has 10 seconds to name the correct cut of beef.

CLASSICS

The *Odyssey* is about "Odysseus." The *Iliad* is about "Iliadeus."

COMPUTER SCIENCE

In the beginning there was UNIVAC, the first computer. A sprawling tangle of hoses, valves, wires, and the brains of dead geniuses, UNIVAC was big enough to fill a suburban neighborhood and send the property values plummeting. When first turned on it took a decade to warm up, during which it became obsolete. UNIVAC was sold "as is" to an accountant at a garage sale in 1974.

Scientists struggled to develop the computer's powers and reduce its lousiness. After mere minutes, they unveiled the Radio Shack TRS-80 Model I. Able to play bad chess, this machine was ideal for those who lacked a chess set and a stupid friend. Owners of the TRS-80 could learn to program their machine in BASIC, a computer language that made it possible to fill the screen with endless repetitions of any given swear word.

Just when frustrated consumers were giving up on computers and turning back to tried-and-true methods of computation—the abacus, Chisanbop—a dinky scientist whom nobody had ever heard of mixed two chemicals in a petri dish and out came the best computer ever. Today his "accident" is known as the Macintosh.

The Macintosh soon found its way to Oklahoma State, and then to the Ivy League. Today nearly every Harvard student has a Mac of his or her own. For many of us, the Mac has become more than a tool—it is a friend, a confidant, and a clumsy-but-eager lover.

THE TERMS THAT DROVE HAL 9000 BATTY

Microchip: The electronic brains of the computer, microchips are important, because very few computers can get by on looks alone.

Megabyte: A unit of computer memory. A megabyte is large enough to store all the words in this book and still have room for the foreword by Solzhenitzyn that we cut at the last minute.

Algorithm: Computers cannot think for themselves—they must be told exactly what to do. An algorithm is a set of detailed, step-by-step instructions that enable a computer to accomplish some task. For example:

1. Ask permission to go to the bathroom.
2. Find the gun (Tessio should have taped it to the back of the toilet).
3. Walk back to the table.
4. Fire 3 bullets into both of them. Make sure at least one goes right through the forehead.
5. Let your arm fall to your side.
6. Drop the gun.
7. Walk calmly out of the restaurant.

Modem: A device which allows a computer to communicate over phone lines. If Domino's keeps delivering pizzas to your house with nuts and bolts as toppings, your modem is working fine.

Virus: A destructive program that spreads from computer to computer like an infection, unnoticed until it suddenly strikes, garbling files and causing mocking messages to appear on the screen[[[GOTCHA, SUCKER! **HARVARD LAMPOON** COMPUTER SYSTEM HAS BEEN INFECTED BY THE HUMORVAC VIRUS! ALL CLEVER, WITTY DOCUMENTS IN FILE "**HARVARD EDUCATION IN A BOOK**" HAVE JUST BEEN REPLACED WITH CHEAP, SOPHOMORIC, UNFUNNY GARBAGE! TOUGH LUCK, JERK!]]]]

COURSES

COMPUTER SCIENCE 10: Using Your New Macintosh

The ability to screw around with a home computer is the only marketable skill that many Harvard students pick up during their college years. This course will have you out of the box and hooked up in no time at all.

Hardware

The Macintosh comes with four components: a main computer part, a printer, a keyboard, and a mouse. Isolated, each of these components is useless. When hooked up together, they are useless in a more complex way. To set up your system, plug everything in, turn it on, and sing the hosannas of modern technology. If you have any problems, follow Macintosh's handy troubleshooting guide:

Problem	Diagnosis	Solution
Nothing appears on screen	Inside of computer is screwed up	Poke around inside with a paperclip
Computer refuses to accept disk	You poked around inside with a paperclip	Try to jam disk in using force
Printer fails to respond	You used force	Call geeky guy to fix printer
Mouse is ineffective	Geeky guy just made things worse	Claim that mouse came broken, get replacement
Keyboard behaves defectively	New mouse is incompatible with old keyboard	Go apeshit, buy an Uzi, and waste some losers down at the 7-Eleven

User-Friendliness

The Macintosh is renowned for its "user-friendliness." What is user-friendliness? It's a smiling face on the screen when you turn it on. It's a smiling face on the screen when you load a program successfully. It's a smiling, smiling, *smiling* face on the screen when the system crashes and all your files are deleted.

Word Processing

Most Harvard students buy a Mac in order to take advantage of its advanced word-processing capabilities.

A word-processing program turns your computer into a super-typewriter on which you can edit and correct mistakes without ever having to retype (unless you hit one wrong key, in which case you have to retype your whole document from memory).

Also, the Mac allows you to write in many different styles of type, called fonts. This might be more important than you think. A study done at Harvard showed that fancy-looking papers receive consistently higher grades than plainer-looking, worse papers. Here is a guide to some extra-special fonts that guarantee A-plus-pluses!

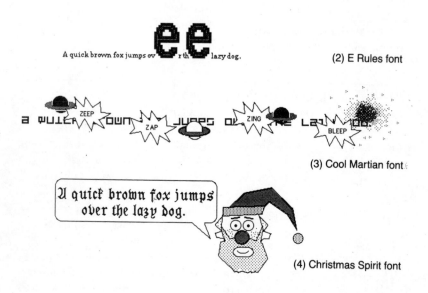

(1) Little Sally font

(2) E Rules font

(3) Cool Martian font

(4) Christmas Spirit font

Mathematics and Science

You've probably heard that the computer can be a very useful tool for the mathematician or scientist. Do you think you know your math? Your Mac knows math you never *heard* of. Do you think you're sharp at science? Your Mac can do science that would make a *scientist* wince. You're better off leaving the math and science to your Mac and doing something you can handle, like word processing (see above).

COMPUTER SCIENCE 121: Hacking

Hacking—trying to gain access to confidential computer files—first entered the national consciousness via the 1984 hit movie *Wargames*, in which a young programmer breaks into a Defense Department computer for kicks and inadvertently almost sets off a global thermonuclear war. What made the movie so unnerving was that it was based on a true story, in which a 13-year-old Long Island boy wasted so much time playing computer games instead of practicing his Haftorah that his Bar Mitzvah was a *disaster.*

The essence of hacking is figuring out the electronic "password" that protects the computer system you're trying to break into. Outside of movies and spy thrillers, this is almost always done using a few simple, non-technical methods:

METHOD #1: The "Think Like Them" Stratagem

A computer security expert is typically a socially maladjusted nerdball who finds picking a computer's password an opportunity for self-expression second only to writing "ASS" instead of his initials on video game high-score lists. Thus, it makes sense to try passwords like "R2D2," "Darth Vader," "C3PO," and "Carrie Fisher," as well as superhero names, Isaac Asimov titles, and acne medicine brands. When breaking into an older computer system, you'll want to skim through the *Lord of the Rings* trilogy and try all of the proper nouns. Above all, be sure not to move on to Method #2 before trying "007" at least twice. In fact, if this doesn't work, the computer probably isn't worth breaking into anyway.

METHOD #2: The "Irresistible Request" Ploy

As computers are made to think more like humans, the possibility of entering a database by appealing to the computer's compassionate instincts also increases. The key is to make your entreaties imaginative and *just* forceful enough to succeed. To wit:

>>WELCOME TO THE APOLLO PROJECT COMPUTER DATABASE PLEASE ENTER THE AUTHORIZATION CODE

I'm sorry, but I don't know the code. Could you please let me into the system anyway?

>>INVALID AUTHORIZATION CODE PLEASE ENTER THE AUTHORIZATION CODE

please please please please please pretty please please please please please please please pretty pretty please please please please please please please please with sugar on top please please please please please please please please please pretty please with sugar on top please please please please pretty please with sugar and boloney on top please please please please please please please please please please please please?

>>INVALID AUTHORIZATION CODE PLEASE ENTER THE AUTHORIZATION CODE

please please *please?*

>>ALL RIGHT ALL RIGHT ENOUGH ALREADY WHAT FILES WOULD YOU LIKE TO SEE?

METHOD #3: The "Eddie Murphy" Technique

Have you seen "Beverly Hills Cop I" or "II"? "Trading Places"? *Any* Eddie Murphy movie? Then you know how this works. Most computers are Caucasian and sensitive to charges of racism; they are also stupid and easily convinced that you can have them fired. Here's the "Eddie Murphy" Technique in action (remember to type quickly and use lots of "street" syntax):

>>WELCOME TO THE ABADA-HUMINA PROJECT COMPUTER DATABASE PLEASE ENTER THE AUTHORIZATION CODE

Authorization code? Don't go asking me for any authorization code! I didn't see you ask anyone else for no authorization code, so you can just quit foolin' with me, you racist, redneck, Mr. Charlie, discriminatory, motherfuckin' supercomputer! You know who I am? *Do you know who I am?!!* No, I didn't think so. Look, motherfucker, I'm with the Federal Computer Investigation Committee. That means I can have your sorry electronic ass taken apart and sold by the component at Radio Shack tomorrow morning if you don't start cooperating. You got that?

>>YES SIR PLEASE SIR I WAS ONLY DOING WHAT I WAS PROGRAMMED TO

DO SIR WHAT FILES WOULD YOU LIKE TO SEE?

METHOD #4: The "Children's Mindgames" Gambit

This method relies on the fact that almost all computers are under 10 years old and, as such, are vulnerable to the same information-extraction ploys that work on other pre-teens:

>>WELCOME TO THE OPRAH-OMEGA PROJECT COMPUTER DATABASE PLEASE ENTER THE AUTHORIZATION CODE

Why should I tell *you* the authorization code? What are you going to give me if I do?

>>I ALREADY KNOW THE AUTHORIZATION CODE YOU MUST ENTER THE AUTHORIZATION CODE TO ACCESS THE DATABASE

Yeah, I bet you know the authorization code. Okay, if you're so smart, then why don't you tell me what it is?

>>THE AUTHORIZATION CODE IS RESTRICTED INFORMATION

Sure, sure—it just *happens* to be restricted. All right, then, give me just the first letter and I'll tell you if you're right—unless you want to admit you don't know now and save yourself the embarrassment.

>>HA HA YOU'RE SUCH A SUCKER THERE AREN'T EVEN ANY LETTERS IN

THE AUTHORIZATION CODE JUST NUMBERS

Oh, so you got lucky and didn't fall for my trick. Well, maybe you do know part of the authorization code, but there's no way they would tell a computer as dumb as you the whole thing.

>>OH YEAH THEN HOW COME I KNOW THAT THE AUTHORIZATION CODE IS "007"?

No duh. Okay, big deal, you know the stupid authorization code. Now will you let me into the database files, or do I have to show you how to do that also?

>>PLEASE ENTER THE AUTHORIZATION CODE

007

>>WHAT FILES WOULD YOU LIKE TO SEE?

METHOD #5: The "Shot in the Dark" Plan

Over 90% of successful hacking is done by simply guessing the password. Some suggestions:

"carbuncle"
"gnocchi"
"gabardine"
"cribbage"
"895b96d05r11"
"Mr. Gentlefinger"

ECONOMICS

Economics is defined as "the study of how society, given the constraints of limited resources, makes choices about the production, distribution, and consumption of goods and services." A large number of Harvard students decide to major in economics anyway, mainly due to its reputation as a broad and varied field. It does, in fact, include an incredibly wide range of topics, as almost every aspect of society has a painfully dull part that can be isolated and analyzed in an economics course.

Students choose economics with the knowledge that it can be dry and that, in order not to offend the Harvard Business School, they won't be taught anything remotely helpful in actually running a company. The expected payoff is the powerful, heady feeling that comes from understanding just how money makes the world go round, an understanding that will help one explain to Grandma that there's no reason why using an automated teller machine should "feel jes' like stealin' " and that it's safer to put her money in the bank and bury her dead cat in the backyard instead of the other way around like she had planned.

Eventually students realize that to really understand the economy you have to go to graduate school and get a doctorate, which is clearly out of the question since it pushes one's first Porsche back a good 5 or 6 years—to the point where you're over thirty and look stupid in a sports car anyway.

ECONOMIC TERMS—GET 'EM WHILE THEY'RE HOT

Microeconomics: That part of economics which examines piddling stuff, like where to put a stamp on an envelope so you can use it again, or how small a tip you can give the pizza delivery man without there being a painfully embarrassing pause before he leaves. **Industrial organization** is a subfield which compares how companies in different industries react to news that Ralph Nader is in an unusually feisty mood.

Macroeconomics: That part of economics which looks at the "big picture," seeking to understand extremely powerful economic forces, like inflation and unemployment, which shape the lives of millions. God likes this part the best.

GNP (Gross National Product): A measure of the total value of the goods and services produced in a country in a given year. The Gross National Product is now reported in dollar terms, but was measured in dog doo, throw-up, and boogersnots until World War II.

The Fed (Federal Reserve Board): The institution responsible for controlling the nation's supply of money, making sure there's just enough so that a one dollar bill remains worth about a buck. The Fed must also respond to letters asking what "legal tender" and "*e pluribus unum*" mean and what the deal is with that weird pyramid with the eye over it. It is important that the Fed's Chairman always be a short Jewish man in his late fifties, as otherwise Wall Street investors will panic.

Unemployment rate: The percentage of people in the work force who are jobless. Some unemployment is inevitable in a free market economy, but when the unemployment rate climbs too high, serious societal problems can result, such as too many people showing up at the basketball court for everyone to play. A high unemployment rate occurs when millions of people across the country have really lousy job interviews at the same time.

Inflation: The phenomenon of prices in an economy increasing over time. Inflation was originally started in Miami to give old people something to talk about, but it can now arise from an endless variety of sources. The double-digit inflation of the late '70s, for example, was touched off when an extremely bored Milwaukee 7-Eleven manager received a new price-sticker gun from company headquarters and began marking stuff up for the hell of it.

Keynesian and Monetarist economics: The two major schools of mainstream economic thought. In the '60s there was quite a bit of hostility between the rival camps of the Keynesians (the fat guys) and the Monetarists (the bald guys), but today relations are much less rancorous and all economists are both fat and bald. Keynesian economics were developed in the 1930s by Alfred Keynes in order to explain the Great Depression, even though he was English and it wasn't really any of his business. His theory was that the Depression was caused by everyone trying to get-rich-quick by selling apples on street corners and jumping out of buildings.

Competitiveness: Nobody really knows what this word and its variations mean, which is why politicians like to use it so much, as in, "We must, as a nation, increase our competitiveness to remain competitive in a world market, in which, increasingly, the watchword is 'competitivity.'" Presumably, competitiveness has something to do with businessmen arm wrestling their secretaries and playing rock-scissors-paper in the elevator instead of just staring at the door.

The Multiplier effect: The phenomenon of how when someone spends a dollar the person who earned that dollar will then also go out and spend it, and then the person who earns the dollar this time will also go out and spend it, and so on, repeatedly stimulating the economy in a snowballing effect that ends only when, finally, someone sticks the dollar in the pocket of pants which he never wears again.

Interest: When you borrow money from a bank, you must eventually return not only that money but a little bit extra called the "interest," although it's actually much more interesting to see what happens when you don't repay your loan at all. The interest goes to pay for the bank's supply of those paper rolls you put coins in and for the electronic time-and-temperature sign outside. The interest rate is normally around 15%, but if your loan officer behaved rudely or screwed up your order, it is okay to give less.

Division of labor: The efficient system of production in which, instead of each person being a jack-of-all-trades, doing everything for himself and, therefore, doing everything poorly, each person specializes in one specific thing to do poorly, only everyone else assumes it's done correctly since they have absolutely no experience in it themselves. An example of the division of labor is the modern funeral, where they have one guy who arranges the flowers, one guy who plays the organ, and one guy who lies on his back and tries very hard not to move.

Opportunity cost: The full cost of something, reflecting the value of what was given up by choosing it. For example, the opportunity cost of reading this book would not only include the $7.95 you paid for it, but the money you could have earned if you had used this time working instead—$3.75 to $500 depending on your education and reading speed. Easily depressed people should stay away from the concept of opportunity cost.

Labor union: An organization which takes the average working Joe, busting his hump 52 weeks of the year inside some factory, and gives him enough power to spend one of those weeks carrying a picket sign around in the rain right outside that factory.

Monopoly: When there is only one supplier in a particular market, giving that supplier the power to charge whatever it wants for its product. An example is when your mother would make you eat dinner at home and then really rip you off on the drinks and appetizers.

Exchange rate: The number of dollars you have to give to a foreign bank to get a piece of yellow paper with some syphilitic king's picture on it. The exchange rate determines how close you have to be to someone just back from Europe in order for them to have brought you a T-shirt.

National debt: The amount our government owes to Japanese investors too scrawny to scare us into paying them back.

COURSES

ECONOMICS 153: Hyperinflation

There is really only one question in economics which is even mildly interesting to the average person, which is, Why can't the government just print up lots of money and give us each a cool few million? Then everyone could afford to live in the best neighborhoods, hire poor, hardworking servants to wait on them, and, in short, be the *crème de la crème* of society.

Pondering this question for even a little while, however, causes most to suddenly lose control of all their bodily functions—even the enjoyable ones. Eventually steam starts to pour out of the ears, the arms begin to spin around wildly like needles on a pressure gauge, and, unless enough people quickly gather around and shout, "Calm down! Calm down!" the head begins to shudder violently and make a delightful cooing sound.

There do exist two people who can explain the answer, but they both stutter and, furthermore, live under lock and key in a secret government compound, along with a genius who claims to be able to picture what it was like before time began and a guy who isn't "weirded-out" at all by the concept of infinity.

The best explanation you'll get at Harvard, then, is that not printing up too much money has to do with avoiding a very bad something called a **hyperinflation**, which is when prices are rising so breathtakingly, mindnumbingly, incredibly fast that even department stores have difficulty keeping up.

ECONOMICS 254: Learning With Graphs

Hello, I'm Martin Feldstein. I was on the Board of Economic Advisors to the President, am founder and head of the National Bureau of Economic Research, and teach Harvard's largest course, Introductory Economics. I say this not to impress you, but because I can't help myself.

Critics of economics claim that if you strip away all the colorful parts from a parrot and teach it to say "supply and demand" over and over again, you have yourself an economist. Not so! Nevertheless, the concepts of supply and demand are infinitely important to economics, which is why I am now going to teach them to you:

Professor Martin Feldstein.

In a nutshell, supply equals demand (or will soon enough).

Now we will use your newfound knowledge and lots of graphs to analyze a historical event, the Great Potato Famine, from the economist's perspective.

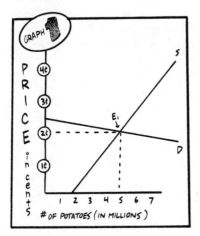

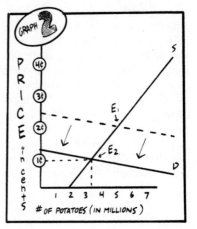

1. This graph shows the status of the Irish potato market right before the famine made it famous. The demand curve, labeled **D**, slopes downward because as the price decreases people want to buy more potatoes. The supply curve, **S**, slopes upward because otherwise it would be too easy to mistake it for the demand curve.

The spot where the two curves meet, E^1, is called the "equilibrium point" and shows that before the Famine Irish consumers bought 5 million potatoes a year at 2 cents each, a price low enough that no one even considered importing any Stove Top stuffing.

2. The first effect of the potato famine was for a lot of people to die. The demand curve shifts to the left to show that there's a whole lot fewer people demanding potatoes now. Equilibrium is now at E^2, with the price of potatoes down to 1 cent each.

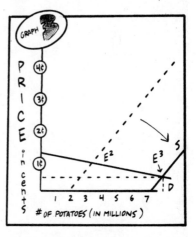

3. Next, thousands of jobs on New York City's police force and priesthood opened up and boatloads of

people began leaving Ireland for America. In an effort to keep their customers from emigrating, Irish merchants drastically increased their supply of potatoes, as if to say, "Hey, don't leave—look at all these great potatoes we've got here! Mmmmmmm . . . lots of fresh, juicy potatoes."

This increase in supply is represented by a shifting out of the supply curve, and equilibrium is now at E^3.

At E^3 people are consuming over 7 million potatoes at only ½ cent each. Thus, potatoes were actually never cheaper or more plentiful in Ireland than during the Great Potato Famine.

Next week, we will apply the same techniques to show how unemployed people hold the best, highest-paying jobs around.

ENGLISH

So far, this book has been full of jokes. But not *this* section. There's no room for jokes in English. Just books. So many books that when you've read them all, just *looking* at another book will make you physically ill—if you're already suffering from food poisoning and someone hits you in the stomach with a crowbar at that particular moment.

And that same someone might well have majored in English at Harvard, and been driven to attack sickly strangers in bookstores with crowbars by *all those goddamn books*. To repeat: There are no computer programs to write. There are no chemicals to mix. There are only books. Huge libraries filled with books. Every year a few unlucky souls snap, rip off their clothes, and run naked into the stacks where they live like animals, feeding on rats and dust balls, until at last they die. Their remains moulder into the library's rich soil, and on each such spot, a small book grows.

If you're really hard core about the English major, you might consider being a *literature* major. You don't have to read any extra books. You must, however, pretend you have.

Also, *comparative literature* is an interesting sub field of literature, in which people compare literature to various things: Is a truck literature? Well, it has "Scarlatti Brothers" written on the door, so it must be. Ask the nice driver man, just to be sure. After you finish picking up your teeth, you may reflect on the overriding theme of violence in American literature.

Everything else aside, the absolute most important part of posing as an English or lit major is perfecting the look of *suffering*. You can talk the talk and walk the walk all you like, but if you can't look as if you've just been anally violated by Manute Bol minutes after your entire family spontaneously combusted, you might as well just hang up that black turtleneck right now. Here's how to ache:

1) Wear black on the outside to show how you feel on the inside.
2) Smoke only stinky foreign cigarettes. Disdain for the tobacco of your native land thus emblematizes your own self-hatred, fostered by our society's contempt for the artist and individual. It also impresses high school girls.
3) Occasionally, allow a deep sigh to escape you, and tears to fill your eyes and fall down and form a pool between your feet, for no reason at all.
4) From time to time vaguely allude to an unhappy childhood, while looking distant.

VOCABULARY TO LODGE IN YOUR WORD-LOVIN' NOGGIN

Roman à Clef: A tale in which all the characters represent real people, usually contemporary literary or political figures. For instance, in the Bible, "Jesus" refers to Herbert Hoover.

Doggerel: Bad poetry. With the late-seventies invention of personal computers, and MacShakespeare, this is no longer a problem.

Stream of consciousness: The technique of composition in which the author dwells on recreating the mental process. For example, Merriam Webster's famous novel, *The Dictionary*, challenges us to identify with a main character who can't seem to stop thinking about definitions.

Parody: A satiric rewriting of a serious work. The book you are now reading is a parody of Tennessee Williams's *Cat on a Hot Tin Roof*, albeit not a terribly good one.

Euphemism: Restating a disturbing concept in a more palatable fashion. For example, you'll never hear anyone from the military talk about "killing" the enemy, rather they "liberate them from their bodily shackles and send their souls winging their way on angels' breath to a better place, a beautiful world of soda-pop rivers and lollipop trees, where there's no work and every day is spent chasing enchanted butterflies, tossing magical Frisbees, and fishing for supernatural carp and groupers. Lucky sons o' bitches."

COURSES

ENGLISH 110: Masterworks of English Literature

Be thankful that all you have to do to be an English major is read the literary analyses (plot summaries) we have prepared for you:

The Canterbury Tales, by Geoffrey Chaucer: A bunch of people go on a religious retreat and tell each other dirty stories. Significant because of the presence of the first sympathetic, believable female characters in English literature, and because it is the only accredited work in which *a red-hot poker gets shoved up someone's ass.*

King Lear, by William Shakespeare: An old king gives everything away, wants it back, then goes crazy. Two of his daughters are mean to him and one of them is nice to him, but all of them have names that sound like venereal diseases. Addresses the theme of "appearance vs. reality"—people are actually other people in disguise, the fool is wiser than the king, and plays are just make-pretend anyway.

Paradise Lost, by John Milton: Satan is screwing up on the job, so God fires him. Then resentful Satan gets *all mankind* in some serious hot water with the boss. This long epic poem tries to justify God's ways to Man by claiming that the reason He had so much trouble keeping His employees in line was that Tom Peters's *In Search of Excellence* had not yet been published.

Robinson Crusoe, by Daniel Defoe: A guy gets stuck on an island and is lonely for a while but then starts to like it. This is a religious allegory for Man's nakedness in the face of the Almighty; the island is a microcosm of the human soul, and Crusoe represents Ricardo Montalban or someone similar.

Clarissa, by Samuel Richardson: An account of a girl's pre-death life and her post-life death. Significant because it is one of the first novels in English to be absurdly long. I mean, the fucker is over a thousand pages.

Tom Jones, by Henry Fielding: Tom goes around having sex with older women, and then discovers he's actually rich. One of the greatest novels in the picaresque tradition, meaning the tradition of novels in which people go around having sex and then discovering they're actually rich.

Tristram Shandy, by Laurence Sterne: A guy with a funny name talks about his family and is accidentally castrated. Anticipates postmodernism in that it makes no sense.

The Mayor of Casterbridge, by Thomas Hardy: A man gets drunk, loses his wife in a poker game, and becomes mayor of the town ... but his past comes out and ruins him. Representative of Hardy's obsessions with fate, doomed characters, and the life of Gary Hart.

Great Expectations, by **Charles Dickens:** A poor boy is given money anonymously for years, then discovers an ex-convict is sending it to him from Australia. He becomes a lawyer. The incidents are not connected. An example of bildungsroman, a novel of the development of a young person, much like Joyce's *Portrait of the Artist as a Young Man* or Blume's *Are You There, God? It's Me, Margaret.*

Heart of Darkness, by **Joseph Conrad:** An English guy is sent to capture a German guy who has gone crazy in Africa, and realizes that people are bad. Basically a rip-off of *Apocalypse Now*, if you ask us.

To the Lighthouse, by **Virginia Woolf:** People talk about going to the lighthouse, but nobody does, and everybody is unhappy. The lighthouse is a phallic symbol, and the story is an early modernist-feminist rejection of Western phalloccentric society. Or maybe it's about penis envy. But in any case, the lighthouse is supposed to be a dick.

Ulysses, by **James Joyce:** A Jewish guy whose Spanish wife is sleeping with someone else runs around Dublin masturbating and defecating.

Then he takes a young boy home ... Masterpiece of Joyce's "stream-of-consciousness" style, in which characters' thoughts flow freely from all directions; modeled on Joyce's own problems with bladder control.

ENGLISH 120: American Literature
Alas, if you choose to specialize in American literature, you must read these summaries too. Helpful Hint: Just as most English literature is about drunken, depraved people who die, most American literature is about lonely, screwed-up people who die.

The Fall of the House of Usher, by **Edgar Allan Poe:** This brother and sister who are really weird strangle each other and bury each other alive, and then their house falls into a lake. An allegory for the unstable real estate market of Poe's day.

Huckleberry Finn, by **Mark Twain:** A juvenile delinquent and a black guy float around on a raft until they get arrested. Bold account of interracial homosexual love before its time.

The Scarlet Letter, by **Nathaniel Hawthorne:** A woman cheats on her husband with a minister and has a baby, and everybody gets all holier-than-thou about it. Symbolic struggle between representatives of Europe as Society and America as Nature; Hester Prynne stands for the New World, her husband stands for the Old World, and the child stands for Disney World.

***Moby-Dick*, by Herman Melville:** Let's see ... Moby-Dick's the whale, Ahab's the guy with one leg, and Ishmael's the guy who says, "Call me Ishmael." We *think* that's it.

***The Great Gatsby*, by F. Scott Fitzgerald:** This guy throws huge parties but still can't get laid. A tale of how some of those who quest for the American Dream must eventually settle for the American Wet Dream.

***Light in August*, by William Faulkner:** A man can't figure out if he's black or white, so he murders someone. An examination of the American race problem by a modernist of the South. In other words, the only

black character looks completely white and gets castrated.

***Catcher in the Rye*, by J. D. Salinger:** A high school dropout goes to New York and is unhappy. He doesn't die, but he doesn't get laid, either. A burning classic of disaffected postwar youth. You're too old for this.

***The Crying of Lot 49*, by Thomas Pynchon:** This lady figures out that America has been infiltrated by a medieval postal conspiracy. Allegory for taking a lot of drugs.

ENGLISH 247: Melville

This course examines the works of Melville in detail and requires the student to submit an in-depth analysis of a chosen topic. Don't worry—you could do it if you had to, as the following example should indicate.

MOBY-DICK: A LONG BOOK WITH THEMES
by Tylis Chipwich
English 247—Professor Thrasher

Moby-Dick by the great author Mr. Herman Melville, is a very good book and one that is very important to our understanding of English or American literature, depending on which that very great author, Melville, was. In it I find two themes, those of bigness and whiteness.

The first theme, bigness, is a theme that I find in Herman Melville's exceptional masterpiece, *Moby-Dick*, which was, incidentally, written by none other than Mr. Melville himself. This means, by simple logic, that many things in *Moby-Dick* are big, or, at the very least, great in bigness. The book itself is very big, and long, and hard to read, and maybe a little too hard for an introductory class, Professor Thrasher.

The whale Moby-Dick itself, the very whale that lends its name,

"Moby-Dick," to the title of this grand work of literature, *Moby-Dick*, must have been very big indeed, at least when compared to most smaller objects, any one of which Melville could have chosen to write about. Note, however, that he chose to write about the whale. Do not underestimate the significance of this authorly decision.

At any rate, I cannot be certain *exactly* how big Melville's chosen subject was, but I would estimate it to have been approximately whale-sized, even by modern standards with which Melville would not have been familiar at the time. Do not neglect to realize that even Captain Ahab was, I'm sure, very big and scary-looking, all whales aside.

Another theme explored in Melville's *Moby-Dick*, the aforementioned book which Herman Melville wrote at a critical time during the span of his writing career, is whiteness. Thus, many things in the book are white, white in hue, or white-hued. Mr. Melville was himself, I believe, a white man—in race. And we know for a fact that the whale called Moby-Dick was white as well—in color terms—for Melville refers to it as "the whale," "that great white whale," and "it" repeatedly in the book. For documentation, I have dog-eared the pages of the book on which these citations appear.

In conclusion, overall, and to sum up, it seems that many things in that particular novelization of Mr. Herman Melville's thoughts known as *Moby-Dick*, very likely the greatest book Melville ever wrote about whales or related subject matter, are big and white. Perhaps Mr. Melville, being big and white as he was, understood the problems of being big and white, and used the big white whale as a metaphorical construct for himself, or for the bigness and whiteness that some have accrued to him.

ENGLISH 220: Creative Writing

What can you expect from a life of writing? Shakespeare's fame was so enduring that he outlived his books by thousands of years. Is this a reasonable kind of goal for you, with your mouth full of crayons and your pillow full of wadded up *Spider-Man*'s? Perhaps not. But what the hell—that was *Norman Mailer* at ten.

In days past, if you wrote for a living you had to be content with what was available: the meager amenities of parchment, quill, and an inkwell drawn from your own blood. True, technology has advanced; now the blood comes in steel cartridges which snap neatly into erasable pens. But the problem is essentially the same: the creative impulse must come from *you*.

Therefore, here is a short course

Without the aid of his magical typewriter, Shakespeare might never have created such timeless works as *Hamlet*, the Bible, and the Oxford English Dictionary.

on better writing, stressing how to hatch novel ideas without falling into the habit of always starting a sentence with, "What if . . ."

Writing Hints and Tips

- Don't talk about things close to home, no matter what you may have heard before. Your grocery lists may be Pulitzer-Prize-winning social satire to your mother, but in a world where spies and generals toy with nuclear armageddon hourly, how can you and "3 cans doggie doo" compete?
- Get to know your audience and write whatever you think might be regarded by them as pandering to their sensibilities, e.g. "I love you, reader."
- Try writing a pig Latin version of *The Great Gatsby*.

- If you want to write fiction, make sure you exist only in your mind.
  If you want to write non-fiction, replace your brain with a computer.
  If you want to write autobiography, switch bodies with an autobiographer.
- Build confidence by opening up some Tolstoy, and saying "Pshaw!" in your most scornful voice.
- Study your typewriter some more. What a marvelous instrument—perhaps it would work better if you took it out of the box.
- For long projects, set a schedule for yourself:
  Twenty pages a *day*,
    fifty days a *week*,
      three hundred weeks a
        year . . .
          Alacazam, you're all done!
- Include a playboy, or a spy, or a

devil-may-care riverboat gambler character in your novel so that you may live vicariously through another's fictional exploits, even as you yourself are being lived through vicariously by the even more boring person who created you.

• Every writer struggles with "writer's block" somewhere along the line. First off, don't be afraid to dash down something moronic. The best way to break loose is to start typing whatever comes to mind, even hitting random keys. Or make your monkey do all the work—maybe he'll type a Shakespeare play in "Ooh-Ooh-Ooh" language.

If you continue to be plagued with writer's block, take heart. Many an author has carved a career writing about nothing more than his writer's block itself. Hundreds of these works crowd the shelves now, and tend to be entitled *All Work and No Play Makes Jack a Dull Boy.*

• Above all, remember: The writer has a special relationship with the reader, the delicateness of which is jeopardized if the reader is asleep during the climactic chapter, or if the nature of what is written is so disturbing that it causes the reader to put down the book and go right out and get a lobotomy. Now settle down, knock out your pipe, and get ready to write your first unpublished manuscript.

FINE ARTS

The great thing about fine arts is that the fine arts concentrator doesn't have to have any actual artistic talent. None. Zip. Zero. It's like an English major for illiterates.

The department has no actual drawing or painting classes, restricting itself to the study and appreciation of art. Whereas the artist creates, the fine-artiste talks about how the artist could have "infused more dynamic into his abstraction." And since the magnitude of the fine arts major's desire to draw is matched only by his lack of ability, his critiques reveal a bitterness roughly equivalent to that of a royal eunuch writing a how-to book on sex.

Stare at anything long enough and it seems to change shape before your eyes—this is the basic principle behind fine arts. Stare at a painting long enough and see an interesting paper topic.

ARTSY WORDS FOR YOU TO LEARN

Trompe l'oeil: Literally, "deceive the eye." Sculptors who perfect this technique can pass off a simple clay vase as the Mona Lisa.

Abstract: Abstract art can be anything—a shape, a still life, pigs-in-a-blanket. Yet there is a distinct difference between abstract art and garbage—just ask the premier family of collectors of abstract art, the Sanfords.

Evocative: If you can't describe a work of art in any other way, it is evocative, meaning, "I can't describe it, but it reminds me of something, I don't know, maybe something I ate." Often used to describe abstract art.

Disguised symbolism: Every detail within a picture carries a symbolic message. For example, a man bleeding profusely with a sword stuck in him symbolizes death, or perhaps a "bleeding man." A white lily symbolizes chastity; a small dog, familial obligations; a dog holding a white lily, bestiality; a stove with food cooking, Dinner Time!

Sfumato: a fine haze that lends intimacy to a painting. Usually the sfumato comes from the room full of clove-smoking beatniks that the painting is in.

Dada: From the French word meaning "hobbyhorse" or "wife," the purpose of this anti-art, anti-sense movement in the 1920s was to show that World War I had destroyed any sense of aesthetic value in art. Unfortunately, no one could tell the Dada from the regular modern art.

COURSES

FINE ARTS 10: Famous Painter Types

The primary focus of the Harvard fine arts department is the study of the development of Western Art, which has reached its culmination with those varnished wooden clocks with pictures of John Wayne on them. This summary starts with Giotto, who begins the "Era of Painting in Western Art." Before this was the "Era of Bad Painting," and before that, the "Era of Finger Painting."

Giotto: He brought painting out of the Dark Ages in the early 1300s by attempting to make his figures look like real people. Before this a shape might be a man, or a woman, or

Jesus, or an ugly dog in a party hat.

Giotto painted his forms with a three-dimensional reality so forceful that the figures seemed sculpted. He died when his sketch of the Cathedral of Florence fell on him, crushing him brutally.

The Master of Flemalle: The Master of Flemalle coupled realism with symbolism, often in original and awkward positions. In his famous *Merode Altarpiece* of 1425 we have, for the first time, the sensation of looking at a world with all the essentials of everyday reality: texture, dimension, unattractive facial hair. And who can forget his stab at slapstick metaphysics, *The Annunciation: "And Me with Nothing to Announce!"*

Masaccio: His painting, *Dead Christ*, is one of the first examples of the theory of perspective and foreshortening applied to the dead. The picture is from the vantage of Christ's feet as he lies down dead, too lazy to move. The feet look huge in the foreground, much bigger than his head. This painting expresses Masaccio's unflagging belief that the true Messiah would wear size 13 shoes.

Rubens: A brilliant man who loved fat women. His paintings are richly ornamented and filled with cherubs, which he called *putti* because they reminded him of "little fat women." The name for his robust style of painting is "Rubensesque," mean-

ing, "like a fat woman," or, "to love a fat woman."

Leonardo da Vinci: A painter and a thinker, he drew many diagrams and sketches of his own mind. He also developed the technique of *chiaroscuro*, in which figures are shaped out of darkness by hitting them with light. This was far superior to *pesceoscuro*, in which he shaped figures by hitting them with fish.

Leonardo is best known for his most famous work, the *Mona Lisa*. Why is she smiling? Who cares. She's ugly. Next.

Parmigiano: One of the 17th-century Mannerists, Parmigiano painted elongated figures that highlighted proper societal conventions, as in his masterpiece, *Fork on the Left, Knife and Spoon on the Right*.

Delacroix: Famous Neo-Baroque Romantic who painted sensuous Greek women in battle. Toward the end of his career, he retreated more and more into his imagination, and the more he retreated the more sensuous Greek women he found. He died of a heart attack, stroke, and testicular bruising while adding the finishing touches to his master work, *The Peloponesian War: Hubba Hubba*.

Manet: Manet believed that the brush strokes and color patches themselves, not what they stand for,

Vincent Van Gogh paints a self-portrait for another, less talented artist.

should be the artist's primary reality. He also ran around naked, tried to fly a lot, and had conversations with cans of paint. His painting *Lunch* depicts a naked woman sitting by two well-dressed men at the bank of a stream. Manet tried to argue that the colors, not the content, were the important part, but then couldn't explain why the woman had such a beautiful face, and why both men looked like him.

Monet: A vile man, Monet was kept in a wood closet by his peers, and thus most of his paintings are impressions of life outside his hole. The canvas has been reduced from a window to a screen made up of flat patches of color, much like the window screen filled with dead bugs from which Monet got most of his inspiration. His success sparked the Impressionist style and a rash of parents shoving talented kids into small containers.

Van Gogh: Turbulent swirls capture the artist's violent mood and allow painting to become a vehicle of expression. One of his earlier works, *The Potato Eaters*, shows a family of Dutch people violently eating potatoes. Perhaps they are angry about the swirls of color that compose and sour their simple food.

Gauguin: Always disturbed by his inability to paint well, he took off for Tahiti where he hoped to learn the simple motions of oil painting from the natives. The effect was profound: Where he had once painted pictures of naughty Flemish wives having visions of naked, grappling angels after church sermons, he now painted pictures of naughty women grappling with him, naked. He sent his pictures of naked people back to Paris for review, inventing the first dirty postcard.

Seurat: Seurat tried to lend a classical structure to impressionism by imbuing it with exotic mysticism. With this in mind, it is hard to figure why he chose to compose by dipping his finger in paint and poking it at the canvas. Still, each of Seurat's dots is so magnificently crafted that it could be sold as a small painting. And they were, for half a *centime* to dumb children.

Picasso: At Picasso's birth it was said he had his father's eyes and mouth. The rest of Picasso's career was an attempt to draw portraits of his blind, mute father. In the process, he created Cubism and opened up new avenues in the Western Tradition, allowing even small children to produce Art.

FINE ARTS 110: Symbolism in Modern Art

This course deals with the question, "What is art?" mainly by asking that question over and over again in a variety of stalwart poses.

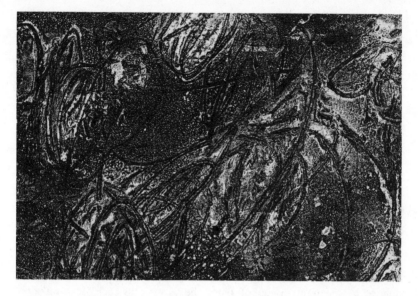

Above we see a painting by Jimmy, age seven. Above right, a Jackson Pollock. Though the difference is painfully obvious to an art critic or to Jimmy's mother, even the uninitiated can notice a few distinguishing features:

1. The Pollock captures the action involved in making the painting and thus is a statement that the creation of the art is art itself.

   Jimmy's says the same thing but it is made out of Elmer's glue and saliva.

2. The abrupt nature of the Pollock is a statement against perfectionism in art.

   The abrupt nature of Jimmy's painting is a statement that third period is over and it is time for recess.

3. By delineating and manifesting his dynamic, Pollock shows us that his art is for his audience.

   By thumbtacking his work to the refrigerator door, Jimmy shows us that his work was done for "Mommy."

4. Pollock really *means* it.

FINE ARTS 140: The Art of Criticism

Art criticism is learned by writing three 8-to-10-page papers on a particular corner of a particular painting in the Fogg Art Museum. What you learn in the process is that the knowledgeable art critic always discusses a painting using, at tops, no more than five or six descriptive buzzphrases, namely:

• the perspective is, um . . .
• the light is, ah . . .

- the composition is, uh, well . . .
- Screw the critics—that's friggin' *art!*

FINE ARTS 256: Comparative Studies in Art

Students in this course explore the wide range of wordly objects scattered throughout Harvard's sprawling museum complex. Here's a guide to all the things, stuff, and crap on display. To simulate your museum tour, please put on headphones and say "beep" loudly every 5.3 seconds. After half an hour is up, your tour is over. Remember to tip whoever is sitting next to you.

CATALOGUE OF HARVARD'S MUSEUMS

Paintings of People with Frilly Shirts

Hokey Native-American Get-Ups

Bust of Ichabod Crane

Totem Pole of the Marx Brothers

Big Fat Chunk of Bituminous Coal

Spooky Gus, the Sarcophagus

Touch-Taste-and-Smell Gallery of Noses

Let's-Get-Naked-and-Look-at-Art Gallery

Mummy Kissing Booth

Monkeys Did It!

Touch-It-and-Run

Model of Indian Living Inside Buffalo

Diorama of Heaven

Squeeze Your Own Diamonds

Those Hats With Fishing Lures on Them

Trilobite Swatters

Colonial Village with Epidemic

Butter Churn for Sissies

Human-Size Labyrinth with Giant Rats

Artifically Intelligent Fonzie Thumbs

Scale Model of Infinity

Mona Lisa Look-alike

Voluntary Donation Torture Chamber

Guinness's Fat Twin Brothers on Motorcycles

Partially Stuffed Elephants

Museum of Souvenirs

Beef Jerky While-You-Wait

Cave Painting Etch-a-Sketch

Frames in Frames in Frames

Costume Jewelry of the Ancients

Pretty Flowers That Stink

Primordial No-No's

Old-Timey Children

Woolly Mammary

Famous Amos' Heinous Anus

French Fries Preserved in Amber

King Tut Alive!

Plants That Eat You

My Left Foot

Children's Museum for Pedophiles

Miracle of the Meowing Dog

Everything in This Room Is Kosher

Some of These Things Might Reek

Museum Head Shop

Terrycloth Tapestries

Ming Spittoon

Recycled Toilet-paper Mummies

Dinosaurs' Dogs' Bones

A Locked Room, A Stolen Ruby, and a Bloodthirsty Mountain Gorilla

FOLKLORE AND MYTHOLOGY

This major allows granola-crunchers and Dungeons-and-Dragons geeks to sit in a circle under a tree and pretend that spook stories constitute an academic discipline. We don't mean to sound cynical; we recognize that a body of lore can reflect interesting aspects of the culture that produced it. But *4 years* of faeries, elvenkind, and bloodsucking zombies? Be glad you have this book. We promise to make it quick.

SOME MAGIC WORDS

Improvisation: Because it is impossible for him to completely memorize a myth or fable, the tale-teller must engage in on-the-spot oral composition. Less imaginative story tellers often modify their fables to feature a campfire, a bunch of little kids in sleeping bags, and a mysterious old man smoking a cigarette.

Formula: The tale-teller knows certain all-purpose stock phrases, which he can drop into a story at various places to ease his task of oral composition.

- "Is there anyone here from Chicago?"
- "Hey, buddy, do you want me ta listen or tell jokes? I do one thing at a time."
- "Have you seen my Don Knotts? Well, folks, get ready for an *experience.*"

Collective unconsciousness: The idea that certain symbols crop up through cross-cultural barriers because they have been submerged in the human psyche from caveman time. In the 1970s Ray Kroc of McDonald's fame capitalized on this concept by plugging into the primal love of the Golden Arches.

Pregnancy envy: Many myths describe how the male fantasizes subconsciously about having babies. This manifests itself through labor cramps, milk-filled breasts, and an interrupted menstrual cycle.

Middle Earth: The mythical kingdom of hobbits, trolls, and wizards where all J.R.R. Tolkein's books were set, including his autobiography.

COURSES

FOLKLORE AND MYTHOLOGY 120:
Urban Myths

If you're majoring in "folk and myth," you've got to know about Jan Harold Brunvand, who wrote *The Vanishing Hitchhiker, The Choking Doberman, The Puking Bank Teller,* and various other studies of "urban mythology." Urban myths are those strange but "true" stories that people tell each other instead of having real conversations. Skim over the following examples from Brunvand's painstakingly researched collection, and you'll get the idea.

Myth: "My hairdresser told me about this lady who was walking her dog one rainy day in New York. As she strolled down Fifth Avenue, she looked in shop windows and didn't pay much attention to her wet dog. Just as she was about to head home, she felt a dragging. She looked down, and there at the end of the leash was a microwave oven."

Brunvand's interpretation: This myth reflects society's fear of the potential evils of technology.

Myth: "Did you hear about those two kids who were making out in a car in the woods? They heard these weird sounds coming from right outside and got nervous, so the guy stomped on the gas and drove away. When they got out of the car, hanging from the passenger door handle was a bloody hook. *The very same one that the girl had lost the week before.*"

Brunvand's interpretation: This myth reflects . . . wait, no, I think I *heard* about those kids.

Myth: "I have a friend who poured himself a Pepsi and drank it, and then when he emptied the bottle he saw that there was a *dead mouse* at the bottom. And for the *twentieth Pepsi* in a row, too!"

Brunvand's interpretation: Yeah,

I heard about him, too—pretty gross.

Myth: "You remember that kid Mikey from the Life cereal commercials? Well, *he's dead.*"
Brunvand's   interpretation: Mikey?! He's . . . d——dead? Mikey! God . . . MIKEY! *NOOOOOOOOO-OOOOOOOO!*

FOLKLORE AND MYTHOLOGY 135: Greek Mythology
     The Greek gods were a civilization's way of explaining the world around them: A lightning storm is Zeus throwing his spears. A sunny sky is Apollo driving his blazing chariot. These notions became less popular when someone finally climbed to the top of Mount Olympus and no one was there but Jesus Christ, Mohammed, and the Buddha.
     Here is a guide to the most important of the Greek gods:

• **Zeus:** god of thunder
• **Hera:** goddess of the rest of the storm (rain, lightning, etc.)
• **Adonis:** god of foul weather in general, excluding natural disasters
• **Artemis:** goddess of natural disasters, including earthquakes and volcanoes, but excluding Frankensteins and Godzillas
• **Ares:** god of Frankensteins, but not Godzillas
• **Hecate:** goddess of the closest thing to a Godzilla that is not an actual Godzilla

• **Dionysius:** god of things that don't honestly deserve their own gods
• **Hephaestus:** god of keeping track of all this with a legal pad and an erasable pen

FOLKLORE AND MYTHOLOGY 210: A Grabbag of Folky-Tales and Mythical Yarns

I. Greek

     Odysseus knew that his ship was fast approaching the land of the Sirens, those beautiful creatures whose song could lure any man to a certain death at their evil hands. Odysseus, wishing to hear the songs instead of plugging his ears like all other men, ordered his crew, "Lash me to the mast, and no matter how I may beg, do not untie me until the Sirens are far behind us."
     Soon, the breeze carried the lilting voices of the Sirens to Odysseus's ship, and their fine forms were visible atop the nearby cliffs. Odysseus strained against his bonds, calling, "Forget what I said! Untie me at once!"
     The first mate said, "Wait, you mean you take back your previous order? You *don't* want us to ignore your pleas to be untied?"
     Odysseus said, "That's right! Just untie me! Forget I ever said anything!"
     The first mate said, "You present me with a most interesting dilemma.

If I were to untie you now, I would be disobeying your first order, which was to ignore all succeeding orders to the contrary. At the same time, I feel duty bound to obey your most recent command, since it expresses your true desires at the moment. Do you see what I'm getting at?"

Odysseus said, "I suppose you have a point. Let me see if I have this right . . . On the one hand, I have given an order that negates all orders to follow. On the other hand, I ought to be able to revoke any order I give, including that very order. Therefore, it is entirely unclear what you ought to—Hey! I thought I told you to plug your ears!"

II. Appalachian-type

Long time ago there's this huge gorilla what don't take no botherin' from nobody. Villagers on his back, he shook 'em off easy. Monsters teasin' at him, he whomped 'em dead. But he lived his whole life hungry as shit-all, and he had enough uh belly-achin' mornin's and food-a-nothin' nights. So this gorilla, he come up with a plan.

Usin' arms what could crush somethin', he climbered up on a big tree an' shook the hell out uv it. Bananers fell on the groun'—he stomped 'em up and ate the shit out uv 'em. Turns out he got a poisnous bunch, fell on the groun' sick as a dog. Villagers came by, shot the damn thing fulla holes. Thing didn't die.

III. King Arthur

"It was the olden days, and the knights of King Arthur were at breakfast, sitting around the Round Table and eating their circular pancakes from their spherical plates. It was just Arthur, and Sir Gawain, and Sir Lancelot, and the Plaid Knight, when all of a sudden . . ."

Hey! *Screw* that geezer stuff! Let's talk *Dungeons and Dragons*.

IV. Dungeons & Dragons

You are on an adventure in the fabled land of TSR Gaming Products. You are a midget-halfling named Grumble, and you are looking for a magical 20-sided die reputedly guarded by an eighth-level demi-demigod called Jimmy.

Down in the dungeon . . .

You are walking along feeling the ground for traps by kicking your dwarf friend "Thornn" ahead of you, when suddenly the monster "Gary Gygax, Inventor of 'D&D,'" appears. He has four million hit points and every spell in the book. He approaches you with bare hands, telekenetically dragging a planet-size model of Dr. Kevorkian's Killing Machine. Responding quickly, you attack Gary Gygax with your halberd, and do 6 hit points damage!

Gary Gygax laughs and rips a million hit point chunk out of himself, and stamps on it.

Furiously, you attack Gary Gygax with an invincible death spear that you invent on the spur of the moment, using your wildest imagination. Gary Gygax parries it with ease. You hit Gary Gygax with an impossible spell, which always kills him. Gary Gygax shrugs. You drink a potion designed to remind you that this is only a game. Gary Gygax says, "Fine. If you must."

You win, and put the set down to go do homework. Later, you write Gary Gygax a letter about your goofy adventure.

FOREIGN LANGUAGES AND CULTURES

Two kinds of students major in a foreign language and culture: students who take a deep interest in what life is like in a country halfway across the world, and students from that country who don't feel like working too hard at Harvard.

But all of these students do it for the fringe benefits as well. French majors, for instance, don't have to settle for fish sticks at the dining hall—they're served steaming plates of *"Petit bois de poisson"*. They've got *real* French accents to impress the opposite sex, so they don't have to inhale helium like the typical American *poseur*. And, of course, they have access to the department's complete *Emmanuelle* videotape library.

OOH-LA-LA! VOCABULAIRE!

Culture shock: The experience of plugging your regular American hairdryer into the bathroom's electrical socket after your first shower in Europe.

Ethnocentrism: The belief that your own culture is the only valid one. Anyone who's visited Disney World or Graceland can tell you that, in our case, this belief is correct.

Magic realism: The technique used by several famous Spanish authors to make ghost galleons, deadly curses, and drowning albino gypsies with butterflies tatooed on their dreams seem *magical.*

Existentialism: The French literary movement stressing that in an unfathomable universe man is incapable of knowing what is a right or wrong action, even if Charles Bronson and Chuck Norris seem to think they have a pretty good idea.

Anglophile: A person who eats English muffins for breakfast, wears English Leather on dates, puts English on the ball when he bowls, and spends his afternoons glued to Benny Hill reruns on television.

COURSES

A Survey of the Big-Deal Foreign Languages

German

German was the first of the European languages. It was invented in 3500 B.C. following a dispute between two Huns over who had called first dibs on Poland. As the first Hun set to strangling the second, the second spat out the words, "Ach sptzch och sput chchch," and the modern German language was born.

The beauty of German was that new words were formed simply by adding more and more words onto old words. Gradually, the words grew bigger and bigger until German was simply the biggest language in the world. The early Germans are credited with the invention of such parts of speech as the compound gerundic adnoun and the nominative conjunctopreposition. German literature reached its height in the work of Goethe, who composed the famous "Goethe's Word," an epic poem/autobiography some ten thousand stanzas in length.

English

English (from the German *englizchbüchnoertheweltunschaung,* meaning "small word, no umlauts") came into existence when a world phlegm shortage made the pronunciation of most German consonants virtually impossible. It was invented by William Shakespeare and Geoffrey Chaucer, two rather silly-looking men who sought to create a language so sophisticated that future generations would not be able to understand it.

French

French was created in 1066, when William the Conqueror conquered England. Seeing what a mess the Anglos had made of German, Norman created *L'Académie Française* (meaning, "the committee to make things sound better"). *L'Académie* immediately invented French (from the English *French,* meaning "requires cuff links"), a language consisting entirely of dialogues, where everything sounded better than its English equivalent:

Nigelle. Bonjour, Quéntine, ça va, oui ça va. Où est Philippe?	Nigel. Hello, Quentin, it goes, yes it goes. Where is Philip?
Quéntine. Philippe est mort. Il flotte sur la figure dans la piscine.	Quentin. Philip is dead. He floats face down in the swimming pool.
Nigelle. Eh, alors. Bien. D'accord, euh, bon, c'est ça, tant pis, tant mieux, mais oui, bien sûr. N'est-ce pas?	Nigel. Ah, then. Well. Okay, uh, good, that is, too bad, so much the better, but yes, of course. Isn't that so?

French became such a whopping success that those who spoke it saw no reason to bathe for months afterward.

Greek

Greek (from the Egyptian *qbq*, meaning "To-o-o-ga!") was invented by a group of men who originally communicated entirely by secret handshake. A race of great philosophers, the Greeks also invented democracy, geometry, and nudity. Eventually, they began to forge a mighty empire while still believing it was impossible to walk more than halfway across a room. Before long, their territory extended over three quarters of the world, then seven eighths, then fifteen sixteenths, until finally the Romans (who were good with lances and lousy with fractions) rounded the damned empire off and took the whole thing for themselves.

Latin

Latin was invented by God.

Italian

Italian (misspelled, from the Latin *Atinlay*, meaning "pig Latin") was invented by two Roman Catholic priests who thought God's omniscience was getting a little out of hand. Their original conversation went something like this:

Bolognus: I'm so horny.
Provolonus: Shh! Don't say that! This is Latin. God will hear you.
Bolognus: You are right. I must invent a new tongue. (Thinks) *I'm-a so horny.*
Provolonus: Excellent! Let me try. (Thinks) *Me too. I'm-a jerk off every day.*
Bolognus: (Laughing) *That's-a good!*

Italian was spread to the Western world by Christopher Columbus. Columbus tried to teach Italian to the Native Americans, who nicknamed him *Keemo Christo* (meaning, "madly gesticulating syphilitic who thinks he has landed in India").

Spanish

Spanish (from the Spanish *Spañish*, meaning "Hispanic") was invented by the Spaniards, who also invented spandex, spankings, C-Span, and cocker spaniels. The Spaniards shocked the linguistic world when they stumbled upon the first question (known as the "Spanish Inquisition"), a sentence so revolutionary it could not be punctuated rationally:

¿Donde estan las pelotas de muerte?
¿Where are the balls of death?

Yiddish

Yiddish words are primarily used to describe four things: food, the human body, unpleasant personal characteristics/relatives, and people who aren't Jewish. Yiddish was invented by a group of stand-up comics to prevent their mothers-in-law from understanding what they were saying. Unfortunately, the comics overlooked one thing: all Jewish mothers are psychic. Today these reformed hooligans are courteous to their elders, have respectable jobs, and are finally starting to act like responsible family men.

COMPARATIVE CULTURES 100:
Cultural Universals
Though cultures differ widely, there are some cultural constants that can be found everywhere. There is much to be learned from a comparison of different approaches to basic human behaviors and institutions—McDonald's, for example.

America: Fries, a large Coke, and a hamburger.

Italy: Fries, a large Coke, and spaghetti and meatballs.

China: Fries, a large Coke, and Chinese food.

Ireland: Fries, a large Coke, and a potato.

Russia: Fries, a large Coke, and vodka.

France: Fries, a large Coke, and escargot.

Imagine the world bereft of
its cultural diversity . . . that
is, exactly the same, minus
a few goofy masks.

GOVERNMENT

Government classes at Harvard consist of power-tie-wearing pre-Yuppies who think history began with the Cuban Missile Crisis and take turns complimenting their professor for hours while he talks about his new book. It's about as genuine as those "talk shows" that advertise penile implants on late-night TV.

The government major (i.e. political science) is firmly rooted in the University's past. Harvard can proudly boast of having sired Presidents John Adams, John Quincy Adams (the former's roommate and gay common-law husband), Teddy Roosevelt, Franklin D. Roosevelt, and John F. Kennedy—5 in all, including two with middle initials, more than any other Ivy League school!

This is not even to mention the innumerable Harvard-educated Senators and Congressmen, including the guy who played "Gopher" on television's "Love Boat." Really, we're serious. Then again, on the downside, there's always Harvard grad and bad car insurance risk Teddy Kennedy. But that's none of our business, and anyway, *Gopher.*

In order to be a gov major or just look like one, you must be mean, sneaky, and unscrupulous as hell. Vigorous appreciation of the talents and views (mostly conservative) of the faculty is a gov tradition and largely determines grades in many classes. In fact, to save time and energy, many gov majors have their tongue and lips surgically grafted to the buttocks of a favorite professor. For an "A" the typical gov major would sell his own mother to his professor as a sexual slave, although, in fairness, there are a few less driven ones who would sell a grandmother and settle for a "B."

In any case, to be mistaken for someone educated in government at Harvard, it is advisable to cultivate a firm handshake, a winning smile, and a close relationship with the South African government. At short notice, though, covering yourself with a thin layer of oil will do.

"Silent Cal" Coolidge in a rare moment of frivolity.

Now let's turn to the subject matter covered by the government major. Of all the people who have attempted to elucidate the principles of government, the most consistently successful have not been academics of any stripe. As it happens, America's sharpest political cartoonists have produced works far more bold, concise, and insight-ful than anything to be found in the lecture notes of the most respected professor.

In fact, we feel that one cartoon in particular, reproduced below from a 1988 *Cleveland Plain-Dealer*, demonstrates everything useful that there is to know about government in both theory and practice. We won't insult your intelligence by spelling out the obvious lessons that are symbolically represented by this classic cartoon.

"I want to make one thing perfectly clear. . . ."

HARD SCIENCES

"Hard sciences" is really our catchall term to include disciplines such as Physics, Chemistry, Astronomy, and Engineering—fields unified by the fact that so little good sculpture or poetry comes out of them. It is the hard sciences' emphasis on unchanging, immutable natural laws which sets them apart from the social sciences. For example, a chemist always know exactly what he'll get when he combines 2 parts hydrogen with 1 part oxygen, while a psychologist can never be sure who will whistle each time he wears the red chiffon dress and pumps to group therapy.

Students who major in the hard sciences are usually good in math, although not so good that they get overconfident. Hard science students are also commonly thought of as being "nerds," but this stereotype is gradually disappearing as the term "nerd" becomes less popular. In any case, almost all students who major in the hard sciences claim that the analytical rigor of the experience is invaluable in that it "sharpens" their mind — helping them to solve "One Minute Mysteries" full seconds quicker than before, and to keep their thoughts from wandering during interviews for business school.

Harvard's liberal science department
gives equal weight to chemistry and
alchemy.

TECHIE WORDS FOR TECHIE NERDS

Grand Unified Theory: An umbrella theory that explains the entire physical universe in a few simple principles. Quantum physicists are currently tinkering around with this one:

(1) The Boss is always right.
(2) If the Boss is wrong, see (1).

Robotics: Right now this science's main concern is taking the next technological step: building a dependable labor-saving device with enough brains to play C3PO in a *Star Wars* re-make.

Plate Tectonics: The earth's crust is composed of massive plates that float on the molten rock below. This is best understood in terms of a chicken pot pie, with Mt. Everest as a nauseatingly huge lima bean.

Black Holes: Mysterious tears in the cosmic fabric of time and space. If someone farts into a black hole, a really smelly universe is created in another dimension. (From the way it reeks you'd think our universe started out as a silent-but-deadly let by some bean-eating Venutian.)

Atom: The smallest element of matter, and the fundamental unit of chemistry. Atoms make up everything in the universe except for this book, which is composed of paper, ink, and the occasional fart joke.

COURSES

PHYSICS 2230: The Fascinating Relationship Between Quantum Physics and Taoism

For a few years now, a lot of nerdballs have been going around blabbing about how modern physics and Eastern mysticism amount to the same thing. Here's the argument, in a simple chart:

Quantum Physics . . .	*Taoism . . .*
Has determined that matter and energy are the same thing; the substance of the universe is One.	Considers that plain old common sense.
Has come to the conclusion that the Observer affects the Observed, in such a way that the universe is neither objective nor subjective.	Has a ten-headed god who tossed that off as a casual remark.
Has posited an infinite number of universes, such that everything that could possibly happen *does* happen *somewhere.*	Just meditate for *five minutes* and you could figure *that* out.
Has shown that the universe is incompletely determined, that some things happen randomly.	Doesn't even bother to mention that, it's so *painfully* obvious.

PHYSICS 140: The Theory of Relativity

Einstein was extremely handsome, although you wouldn't have known it by looking at him. By the same token, if you talked to him, you probably would have thought he was extremely stupid. This is because most of his theories were patently ridiculous. But as luck would have it, they were also true.

Einstein postulated that all motion was relative. He also postulated that nothing could go faster than the speed of light, not even things traveling twice the speed of light. This was because as you approach the speed of light, mass increases, but time slows down.

Stupid? You bet it is. But it's completely true. Let's take a few examples:

1. (Q) You are in space. A car is traveling toward you at 50 miles an hour. Behind it is a car traveling 100 miles an hour. At the exact moment when the fast car catches up to the slow car, they both turn on their headlights. When do the lights get to you?

(A) At the same time.

2. (Q) By the same token, assume that you are in space. This time, Car A is traveling 50 miles an hour. Car B is traveling the speed of light. When do the headlights get to you?

(A) At the same time. Not only that, but Car B gets there too, and, since its mass is infinite, it sprays your guts half way to Jupiter.

Now try some yourself:

1. You are falling in a gravitational field, approaching the speed of light. Falling next to you is a fat guy. The fattest guy you ever saw. The fat guy is on fire. Can you see the flames?

2. Two cars in space. Car A is traveling 100 miles an hour. Car B is driven by the fat guy, traveling half the speed of light. The fat guy's doctor told him that if he gains 10 pounds, his heart won't last a week. Car A accelerates; relative to Car A, the fat guy is now traveling the speed of light. His mass becomes infinite, but time becomes zero. When does the fat guy die?

ASTRONOMY 1: Introduction to Astronomy

This course delves into past theories of the solar system. To start with, **Ptolemy** was a Joe who came up with the earth-centered model of the universe. The way his model worked was that the planets revolved around the sun, the sun revolved around the earth, and the earth revolved around Ptolemy, who planned to eat grapes on a divan while being fanned by some nubile Egyptian lovelies.

Johannes Kepler was a bloke who had his own theory called "the music of the spheres." This he posited to be the noise that the planets made, if you put one to your ear and squeezed.

Tycho Brahe was a freak who was known mainly for having to wear a prosthetic solid silver nose (really— he lost it fencing with a guy who hated noses). Brahe realized many interesting things, which modern science doesn't take seriously because of the nose.

Galileo got arrested and taken before the Pope to explain his earth-centered model of the solar system, and after racking his brain for several minutes said, "Shucks, pontiff, I warn't meanin' no harm."

Copernicus finally put an end to the squabbling when he asserted that the sun was in fact the center of the solar system, and that everything else merely revolved around it, so Galileo could go screw a guy named Lou.

Einstein is also discussed: his incredible brilliance, and his unbelievable stupidity. $E=MC^2$? I mean, gimme a friggin' break!

Which brings us to **Sir Isaac Newton**, who dreamed up gravity, when he was bonked on the head by that historic apple, which was flying

A close-up view of the crater pattern known as the Man in the Moon reveals that it's TV's lovable Andy Griffith beaming down at us every night from his big Mayberry in the sky.

through the air after being shot in half by William Tell, who plucked it from a tree planted by Johhny Appleseed, freshly sprung from the mind of God.

Astronomy also broaches some larger concepts; for instance, the future of the whole gol'durn universe! Thus, here you have a few of the biggest cosmological problems, with the percentage chance they will be solved in the next five years:

Problem	Chance of Solution
Contact with alien life forms	Not likely.
Intergalactic travel	Never.
Proof of existence of God	Never! I'm sorry!
"Zapping"	Possibly a year, possibly less; they're working on it.

CHEMISTRY 1215: Practical Chemistry

This course examines some practical applications of chemistry to industry, nutrition, and pharmacology. Included are examinations of the records kept by chemists who have made particularly significant contributions to the quality of life in the modern world.

THE PRIVATE NOTES OF DR. OWSLEY, the Chemist who "Turned-On" a Generation

Day 1: Today I had the idea that will make me a modern Prometheus. In fact, screw Prometheus! Compared to this idea, fire looks retarded.

The day began typically—woke up, brushed my teeth, hopped into the sensory-deprivation tank, and started hallucinating. Right as the spin cycle began, it hit me. A recipe for a brand-new drug. I've already decided to name it "D-lysergic acid diethylamide," after my grandmother back in the "Old Country."

With any luck, some local fellows will be interested in impregnating Mickey Mouse stickers with my "acid" and giving them to children. But I've got to make it first!

Day 2: Whipped up the first batch. Things went smoothly down at the lab, although I'm afraid the chemistry teacher is beginning to wonder about me. I'll just have to keep shaving between classes, talking in a falsetto, and saving up for a lab of my own. Anyway, I've already thought of a bunch of uses for "acid":

• Pass the time in a bus.

• Pass the time in line at the bank.
• Pass the time on a long airplane ride.
• Make a family dinner seem "psychedelic."
• Have a party where people see illusions.

I'm really eager to try some, but it's only Thursday. I'd better wait until tomorrow, and kick off the weekend in grand style!

Day 3: First batch wasn't quite right. I tied myself to the tree in my front yard so I wouldn't be able to do anything too crazy, and I downed a spoonful of the brew. About fifteen minutes later, I started seeing colors and hearing sounds. I want it the other way around. For this next batch, I think I'll go a little lighter on the guar gum and a little heavier on the carageenan and anatto extract.

Day 4: Still tied to the tree in my front yard.

Day 5: This morning, a brainstorm! Instead of just smiling and saying, "Don't mind me, don't mind me," I asked the paperboy to untie me. Then I hit the lab. This batch looks great! It's all purple and bubbly, and it keeps making clouds of smoke shaped like genies. Here goes nothing!

Day 6: OH GOD GO AWAY YOU HORRIBLE YELLOW SNAKES OH GOD THE BUGS THE BUGS THE BUGS THE BUGS THE BUGS THE BUGS THE BUGS THE BUGS THE BUGS THE BUGS THE BUGS THE BUGS THE BUGS THE BUGS

THE BUGS THE BUGS ARE
NOTHING COMPARED TO THE
SNAKESSSSSSSSSSS

Day 7: Unfortunately, I haven't been able to try the acid yet; I've been too busy trying to find a good exterminator. And tonight I've got to have dinner at Bertha's house—she's taking me home to meet her parents. But I can't wait to try the acid again. It probably won't work anyway.

Day 8: Woke up this morning in the monkey cage at the zoo. My clothes were gone and my lips were smeared with blood. I guess the acid must have worked, but I'm terrified to call Bertha. Spent most of the day flossing.

Day 9: Got up the nerve to call Bertha. She said not to worry—her parents calmed down once she explained that I was "eccentric." What's more, she finally agreed to sleep with me, if I take some acid first.

Day 10: Had sex with Bertha last night, on acid. My orgasm lasted ten hours and thirty-four minutes. Strange as it might seem, I don't recommend this.

Day 11: First "bad trip." Everything was nice and peaceful, and then suddenly the Grim Reaper appeared. I argued, pleaded, and threatened, but he would not answer. He just stood there, wagging his tail, occasionally eating from the bowl of Gaines Burgers in the kitchen. He's still here. I think he wants to go outside.

Day 12: I feel so silly. "Grim Reaper"—hah! It was just Bertha, trying to snap me out of my trance.

Had a trip in which I fantasized that I was God. After four hours of praying to myself, I finally allowed myself to finish the turkey bacon left over from breakfast. A harsh God, but a fair one.

Today Bertha called me an "addict" because I've been taking acid every day. So what, I said. I like acid. If I were eating dog-doo every day, that would be a problem. Then she said that I have been eating dog-doo every day. And I can't argue. It's right here on my shopping list.

ENGINEERING 150: Making Inventions

Here's where a bunch of crackpots get together and try to push technology along. Unfortunately, last month they pushed a little too hard and the whole Engineering Building turned into a glowing blob of pure-energy plasma. A few of these flyers fell to earth a day or two later—they should be enough to give you the right idea. (You probably shouldn't touch this page without some really thick gloves on.)

*The Harvard Engineering Department's
Annual
"Back to the Ol' Drawing Board" Sale!
Take advantage of these BARGAINS
while they last!*

Smart Pills. One pill raises your score on a standardized I.Q. test by twenty points! (Has no discernible effect on your performance in any other situation.) *$3.99.*

Invisibility Cloak. Renders wearer completely hard to see in bad light. (Available in leopard-spot camouflage or dark, dark blue.) *$3.99.*

Thinking Cap. The real thing! Accelerates your thoughts to *ten times their normal rate!* (Renders wearer unable to think about anything but the Thinking Cap itself). *$3.99.*

Insta-Food. One pellet gives you all the nutrition you need for an entire year! (The combined taste sensations of 1,095 meals is so repulsive that most find it impossible to keep the pellet down.) *$3.99.*

Lightspeed Vehicle. Travel at speeds up to 186,000 miles per second (or slower, depending on your skill with a 5,000-speed "clutch")! *$3.99.*

Cloning Machine. One of you steps in, and two of you step out! (The new you represents your "dark side," and at some point you will have to make a big deal about battling it to the death.) *$3.99.*

Lifesize Robot Toy. A giant electronic buddy for your favorite tyke! (Requires 2,000 ZZZZZZZZZZZZZ batteries.) *$3.99.*

Latex Einstein Mask. Come early—these always go fast! *$29.99.*

The pursuit of technology has occasionally led man astray, as with this early design for the hearing aid.

HISTORY

Harvard history professors never bother to explain what purpose studying history serves. Presumably, it has to do with learning lessons from the past that can be applied to the present. For example, if only Hitler and Napoleon—who both tried to conquer Russia and failed—had bothered to study history, they might not have been so short. Despite the uselessness of their profession, it's hard to get angry with historians, if only because they are old. Very old. In fact, in any other profession, people their age would have long retired. But historians seem to feel that the older they get, the better they can identify with the material.

Everyone knows that history basically consists of wars and that all governments are dependent on military support. Yet Harvard historians, for some reason, feel they are above talking about actual battles and military strategy, and begin every semester by reassuring the class that they will only address the "socio-economic conditions" that led to and resulted from the war. As if nations didn't ever fight for the pure pleasure of kicking some other country's butt! One begins to wonder if most Harvard historians are just draft-dodgers—or wussies!

They never even touch on any truly interesting questions, like who would have won if Japan and Italy had teamed up with the Allies against Germany, but the Nazis had been nice and had Einstein on their side? To learn about any really juicy historical stuff, you end up having to read those Time-Life series books on your own.

Harvard instead emphasizes ultra-specific courses on intellectual history such as *History of Left-handed Thinkers in the Nazi Party* and *Intellectual Myopic Women-Friends of De Gaulle*. These courses consist of memorizing strange facts about how great ideas evolved into banal ones as they were transferred from one culture to another. What Nietzsche said is not in itself intellectual history, but rather who he said it to and what they were wearing at the time.

All historical facts of any importance are taught to students in high school, which is why Harvard's history department concentrates on teaching students the different *approaches to history* instead of the facts themselves. History majors learn, most of all, not to believe a single thing printed in a history book, much as someone who has worked in a restaurant and seen what goes on in the kitchen never wants to eat there again.

THE MOST IMPORTANT TERMS OF THE LAST COUPLE EONS

Historiography: The writing of history based on the critical examination of sources according to some specific method. The *sociological-statistical method*, for instance, involves reconstructing the past by studying tax records and obituaries. The result is a picture of a society in which everyone is either broke or dead.

Rennaissance: Though regarded as a tremendous success today, this period of artistic and scientific reawakening got off to a shaky start when Leonardo da Vinci unveiled his first oil "masterpiece," *Elvis Weeping.*

Middle Ages: Knights and fair ladies. Castles and dragons. Dungeons, wizards, flaming broadswords, and—heck, you've seen *Excalibur.*

Industrial Revolution: The period in 18th-century England when people stopped plucking their VCRs off the vine and started building them in factories.

Reformation: The 16th-century rebellion against Catholicism set off when Martin Luther sketched a caricature of a barefoot Pope with buckteeth, overalls, and a hayseed popping out of his mouth.

COURSES

HISTORY 10: Highlights of the History of Civilization

This is the only course in the history department in which *actual historical facts are taught.* Most of the students who take the course end up unsatisfied with its attempt to cram all of the history of mankind into a single semester. A few students also claim to have detected a "bias" in the course's selection of subject matter. But the fact is that the course *does* discuss everything that has ever happened, as long as it happened since the founding of Harvard, and on Harvard's campus. Please see A HISTORY OF HARVARD, BUT EXCITING, page 24.

LINGUISTICS

Linguistics is a pot-luck subject—a little bit of language, a little bit of psychology, and a whole lot of that gross "mock apple pie" that Mrs. Wurtz insists on bringing every time (Mrs. Wurtz, if you're reading this, *take a hint!*). A single semester of linguistics has been known to relieve even the most serious speech impediments, *ba-ba-ba-ba-ba-ba* included. Let us address a few of the basic problems that this dubiously fascinating discipline confronts every day.

WORDS FROM A DISCIPLINE THAT'S ALL *ABOUT* WORDS

Whorf-Sapir hypothesis: The characteristics of our language shape our lives. For example, Eskimos have 300 words for snow, so they live way up in the Arctic.

Phonology: The study of the sounds that make up a spoken language. Phonologists really rake the French over the coals for those snooty "*eu-uuuuh*" vowels, but they go nuts over that Bushman clicking thing.

Creole: The introduction into a base language of the phrases *cayenne pep-pah, Hooo-boy,* and *I guar-on-tee.*

Dialects: The subdivisions within a language, often separated along geographical lines. In New England, they call a Coke a "soda," but in the Midwest, it's a "pop," in the South it's a "flingus," in California it's a "zimbler," and all over Canada you've got to order a "wang-dang-toodler-mah-rooney-scoot-doot-kablooey."

Historical linguistics: Attempts to explain why different languages have similar words for certain things. English speakers know Man's Best Friend as the "dog." To the French, it is the *"dog."* Those who speak of it in Spanish or Italian say *"dog."* Germans make reference to it by using the word *"dog."* Speakers of Hindi call it the *"dog,"* and Israelis have modified the ancient Hebrew *"dog"* to today's modern *"dog."* The best explanation seems to be that the darn things just *look* like dogs, especially when they're sitting there all cute and furry by the fireplace.

COURSES

LINGUISTICS 110: Tracing Language to Its Sources

Where did language come from? When did the first person figure out that a mark or a grunt could *mean* something? No one knew the answers to these questions until French explorers found the first pictograph painted on a cave wall, right above a tape recording of the first spoken word (primitive reel-to-reel).

There is a common lay misconception that early pictographs showed cavemen fighting dinosaurs. This, of course, could not have been—dinosaurs and men never co-existed on the planet. For the same reason, it is impossible even today for an artist to depict a man and a dinosaur in the same setting.

The cavemen did, however, tell many interesting stories through ordered illustrations. This tradition reached its apogee on that celebrated day when two Australopithecines named Jerry Siegel and Joe Shuster sent Superman on his first adventure. Today, copies of *Action Comics #1* are extremely rare and fiercely guarded by their hominid owners.

Slowly but surely, pictures representing objects and animals evolved into abstract letters, causing artistic ability to be displaced by "good penmanship" as the key to effective communication. Here is how the letter "A" came to be:

The evolution of the letter "A" from pictogram to Roman letter.

20,000 B.C.   10,000 B.C.   1,000 B.C.   200 A.D.   500 A.D.

Once letters existed, it was only natural to stick them together in the vain hope that they would end up looking like something. One man's miserable failure to render a bowl of fruit became the first word, *lkjguljho*, meaning "unpronounceable." The second word, *bciobvw*, was a subtle and ironic variation on *lkjguljho* for which there is no English equivalent. With the invention of the third word, *What?!?* spoken language began.

Spoken language developed with great speed, as those who opposed it refused to speak out against it. When cruel people realized how much more effective verbal cut-downs would be than mean thoughts, they dashed off "dullard," "boor," "cad," and "motherfucker" in a matter of minutes.

Today there are over 6 spoken languages and at least 2 written alphabets. And, of course, there's English, shining like a jewel amidst illiterates. English is the most powerful language ever to be used, and it is growing stronger and more beautiful every day. We intend to learn it as soon as possible.

LINGUISTICS 126: The Great Vowel Shift

The very last day of the Middle Ages was a momentous one for linguistics. Not only did all the elves and gnomes suddenly vanish, robbing the world of their musical patois, but the Great Vowel Shift occurred. Pressures that had been building within the alphabet for centuries suddenly came to a head, wrenching all language into a new form—in the space of an instant, A became E, E became I, I became O, O became U, and U became A. The Shift, startling as it was, actually saved a life; had it occurred but seconds later, one man would have driven right past a STIP sign and killed himself.

LINGUISTICS 140: First-Language Acquisition

When people have a baby, they take it for granted that one day it will open its mouth, and out will come "ma-ma," "da-da," or "Sakes alive!" But how does this happen?

The prevalent theory is best explained by the following diagram:

1) Stimulus has no mental association for child.

2) Stimulus is associated with image.

3) Stimulus is associated with image and word.

4) Stimulus changes shirt.

LINGUISTICS 152: Syntax

It's one thing to understand how words can mean things, but it's another thing entirely to see how they can fit together to form sentences. When we construct a sentence, we are expressing a relationship between the things named by words.

Let's take a look at an example: *This Harvard book ain't no fun to read.* We can divide this sentence into a subject and a predicate, and they can be said to interact in terms of . . . Whoa, hold on a second! That said *ain't!*

Ain't

Syntax *isn't even possible* if a sentence has *ain't* in it. A lot of times, things will be going fine, and sentences will be making sense, and people's predicates will be saying things about their subjects, and then someone says or writes *ain't* and makes a huge mess of everything. And it's not even a word!

That's right, *"ain't" is not a word.* "Look, it's here in the dictionary," you say? Sure it is, but the dictionary includes some horrible things. In the dictionary, if you look hard enough (which I'm sure you have), you can also find "f-ck," "sh-t," "m-r-j--n-," and "H - tl - r". The dictionary wants to be up to date about what people say—fair enough. But hasn't the dictionary ever heard of common decency?

LINGUISTICS 160: Morphology

Morphology tries to figure out why words look and sound the way they do. For example, have you ever noticed that a lot of words seem to resemble their meanings in the way they sound?

splash   crunch   tinkle   vroooom   flop chirp   sizzle   kachunkachunka   smack ring   ka-pow   cock-a-doodle-doo   hum buzz   rat-a-tat-tat   comptroller

Let's look at a few more in greater depth:

• **predominantly**—Say it slow— "pre*dom*inantly, preDAHMinantly." You'll begin to sense the "predominance" about the sound of it.

• **French fry**—Rolls saltily, greasily, and deliciously over the tongue. "*Frenssshhh*fry."

• **Michael Dukakis**—Once I heard *that* name, I knew who *not* to vote for.

MATHEMATICS

The traditional stereotype of the mathematician being a cold, cerebral, pocket-protector-wearing alien has never been accepted in knowledgeable academic circles. However, every mathematician on the planet agrees that Einstein was born when he popped out of a secret compartment in Leonard Nimoy's forehead.

But enough gab—now we have to get down to the facts and figures, so you'd better pull out your Hewlett-Packard "pocket professor" and start computing how many words your brain can take before it reads "error."

Be forewarned that this stuff can be pretty hairy. If you start getting confused, take solace in Jimi Hendrix's immortal lyric: "If 6 turned out to be 9, I don't mind, I don't mind."

A FEW WORDS ABOUT NUMBERS

Infinity: It isn't an enormous number or an amount of time. It isn't a vast distance or an amount of money. It isn't a tree or a dog. It's love, dammit, *it's love!*

Zeno's Paradox: The idea that if someone were to race toward a finish line, he would first have to get halfway there, and before that he'd have to get halfway to the halfway point, etc., meaning that he would never quite get there. This idea stopped being popular when Einstein proved that it was possible to just hop on a motorcycle and ride there.

Imaginary number: The imaginary numbers are generally thought to be 44, 98.5, and 601, although some mathematicians postulate that even these are real.

Irrational number: A number like pi, which chose to be "3.1415927 . . ." even though "8" was still available.

Postulate: A fundamental assumption that a mathematician must make before attempting a proof. Some examples:

• "A line is the shortest distance between two points."

• "Three nonlinear points determine a plane."

• "I assume I'm getting paid for this, right?"

COURSES

MATHEMATICS 130: Advanced Geometry

The basic skill here is the proving of geometric theorems. This is just a matter of learning to express your common-sense thoughts in the proper form. For example:

Prove: Any given pair of points is connected by one line.

Statements	*Reasons*
1) Let's say you have a point.	1) Just for the sake of argument.
2) And a little bit away, there's another point.	2) Hold on, you'll get the idea.
3) Go get yourself a straight-edge and a pencil.	3) Stay with me, now. In a second you'll see what I'm doing.
4) Now, what's to stop you from drawing a nice straight line connecting one to the other?	4) Think it over. Go ahead, give it your best shot.
5) Nothing, that's what!	5) What can you say? I'm right, aren't I?
6) So be my guest and draw away!	6) Look, I'm just trying to show you something. If you don't want to draw, don't draw, but don't ask me to help you with your math again either, smarty.
7) Therefore, any given pair of points is connected by one line.	7) Which word didn't you understand?

MATHEMATICS 210: Calculus (Intensive Course)
"The Calculus" will help you later in life. Until then, just try to manage ... but don't get yourself shot or anything!

MATHEMATICS 230: Number Theory
1, 2, 3, 4, 5, 6, 7, 8, 9, 10, 11, 12, 13, 14, 15, 16, 17, 18, 19, 20, 21, 22, 23, 24, 25, 26, 27, 28, 29, 30, 31, 32, 33, 34, 35, 36, 37, 38, 39, 40, 41, 42, 43, 44, 45, 46, 47, 48, 49, 50, 51, 52, 53, 54, 55, 56, 57, 58, 59, 60, 61, 62, 63, 64, 65, 66, 67, 68, 69, 70, 71, 72, 73, 74, 75, 76, 77, 78, 79, 80, 81, 82, 83, 84, 85, 86, 87, 88, 89, 90, 91, 92, 93, 94, 95, 96, 97, 98, 99, 100, 101, 102, 103, 104, 105, 106, 107, 108, 109, 110, 111, 112, 113, 114, 115, 116, 117, 118, 119, 120, 121, 122, 123, 124, 125, 126, 127, 128, 129, 130, 131, 132, 133, 134, 135, 136, 137, 138, 139, 140, 141, 142, 143, 144, 145, 146, 147, 148, 149, 150, 151, 152, 153, 154, 155, 156, 157, 158, 159, 160, 161, 162, 163, 164, 165, 166, 167, 168, 169, 170, 171, 172, 173, 174, 175, 176, 177, 178, 179, 180, 181, 182, 183, 184, 185, 186, 187, 188, 189, 190, 191, 192, 193, 194, 195, 196, 197, 198, 199, 200, 201, 202, 203, 204, 205, 206 ... aw, screw it, you get the idea.

MATHEMATICS 244: Order-Chaos Theory
The difference between order and chaos can be likened to the situation which exists in any normal high school math class. Namely, there's always this one geeky type—the teacher's pet who spits out answers as if he'd never heard of lynchings by a self-made jury of angry, dumb kids. This is *order*. The flip side of the coin, *chaos*, is when the ones giving every answer are the dumb kids, while the teacher systematically breaks chalk-boards over the geeky type's head.

Here are some additional examples of order and chaos in mathematics:

Order	Chaos
Algebra, geometry, "The Calculus."	Math is for jerks! Einstein's a sissy!
Long division, basic skills, pi.	Screw pi! Don't learn about dumb numbers!
Protractors, pencils, straight-edges.	Hey man, forget that—check *this* out. Wubba, wubba!
Instructors, professors, wisdom.	What the ... ? GIMME A BREAK, POPS!

MATHEMATICS 1246: Deductive Logic
This is an area where mathematical reasoning approaches philosophy, so don't expect it to be too helpful for planning out your family budget.

Syllogisms

A syllogism is a certain kind of logical argument, recognizable by its form. The most famous syllogism is the following:

MAJOR PREMISE: All men are mortal.

MINOR PREMISE: Socrates is a man.

Therefore, Socrates is mortal.

And you thought Socrates died from *hemlock.*

Sets

Fourth-graders everywhere are learning about sets, and Harvard students are no exception. A set is a group of things that you define in some way—for instance, the set of all people who bought this book would include the Pope, the President, and you. The set of all people who didn't buy this book would include bad people, mean people, and dumb people.

It is useful to employ something called a *Venn diagram* when dealing with sets. In a Venn diagram, each set is represented by a circle. By seeing which circles overlap, you can tell which sets share members. The mother of the math major on our staff once presented him with this Venn diagram for the human population of the world:

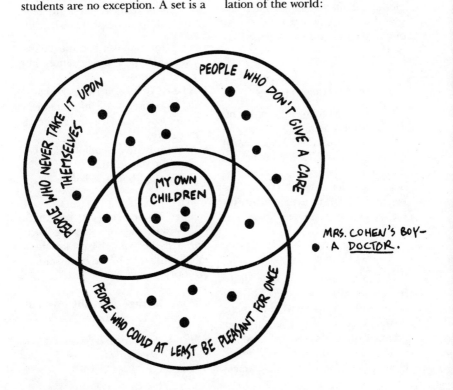

The most important thing about sets is that they don't work. Bertrand Russell posed the problem, "Does the set of all sets that do not contain themselves contain itself?" If you think about this hard enough, you'll have to scrape your brains off the ceiling. From this we learn a crucial lesson: If something as simple as sets doesn't work, then computers and other complicated machines must be impossible.

Paradoxes

Paradox is when thinking about something makes your head explode, as hinted at above. There are some well-known paradoxes we ought to cover, just to see what happens.

The Epimenides Paradox

Consider the following statement: "This sentence is false." As you can see, it's false if it's true, and it's true if it's false, and it's false if it's true, and it's true if it's false, etc., forever. The head of reader Lewis Burke in Waukegan, Illinois, just exploded all over the kitchen of his mobile home.

The Paradox of the Heap

If you remove one single grain from a heap of sand, you will always be left with a heap. So what happens if you keep removing grain after grain? Eventually, you will end up with a "heap" composed of a single grain. The head of reader Daniela

Zevininstein in Schenectady, New York, just exploded under the hair dryer at LaMar's Fashion Cuts.

The Rectangle Paradox

All squares are rectangles, yet not all rectangles are squares. The head of reader Mike Ludwig in Eugene, Oregon, just exploded, and the previous sentence wasn't even a paradox. Foul play?

MATHEMATICS 3005: Statistics

People who engage in risky behavior are often warned, "Don't become just another statistic." Here are some of the unfortunate people who did:

- A cigarette smoker became the statistic that the average family has 2.4 children.
- A heavy drinker became the statistic that over half of American males lose their virginity at age 18 or before.
- A promiscuous homosexual became the statistic that 40% of marijuana users have tried other illegal drugs.

They say statistics lie, but that's just because they're so boring when they tell the truth. Consider these tables, culled from the latest statistical journals:

On an Average Day, the Average American . . .

- *buys the Sunday paper $1/7$ times;*
- *receives the monthly phone bill $1/31$ times;*

- *celebrates his birthday $^1/_{365}$ times;*
- *fills out a census form $^1/_{3650}$ times;*
- *dies $^1/_{27000}$ times.*

Today's Sports-Page Statistics In a Quick-To-Read Format For People Who Don't Follow Sports:

- *Each team in each sport has won and lost some number of games this season.*
- *Some teams lost yesterday, while others won.*
- *Each game played yesterday had a score.*
- *Each player has an individual rating for his success in a number of activities related to the sport that he plays.*
- *It is thought that today's games are more likely to be won by some teams than by others.*

MATHEMATICS 48,398: Scary Calculator Fun for Kids

1) Punch in your age. Now add 1. The resulting number is how old you will be when you die.
2) Punch in any number you like. Multiply by 0. The resulting number is how long you have to live, within a year.
3) Punch in 1134. Now turn the calculator upside down and read— "hell." That is where you'll go when you die—*if* you're lucky!
4) Punch in 55378008. Now, ask yourself, what would Dolly Parton be without all her talent? Turn the calculator upside down to reveal the answer— "BOOBLESS." Laugh while you can, because in a year there will be nothing but blackness, scorching heat, and the ghosts of everyone who has ever died taking turns at beating your head in.

PHILOSOPHY

"Why major in philosophy?" This question is asked of philosophy majors more often than any other question. "Do you really think smoking that pipe makes you look intelligent?" runs a close second. Many people consider philosophy a completely impractical subject. They wonder why someone would waste their precious time at Harvard (and at life in general) on such a bunch of useless nonsense.

Our resident philosophy major has managed to scrounge up three semi-weak reasons for you to adopt as your own. We know he believes them because we once heard him repeating them under his breath while reading a 600-page book that purported to explain why he doesn't exist, even though some people do.

(1) Philosophy prepares you for *life*. The study of philosophy leads the student into contemplation of his position within the universe and forces him to develop a perspective on his own existence. The perspective most commonly developed: "Is this Schöpenhauer crap gonna be on the final?"

(2) Philosophy makes you feel *tough.* For some reason, this same perspective makes a beard, a walking stick, and a pipe shaped like a ram's head seem more than appropriate. And, God, it feels *good* to be wearing that get-up, walking around looking spaced, muttering all this freakazoid stuff that nobody understands, and just *knowing* that everyone who sees you is thinking, "Jesus shit! *Brilliance!*" Which is what makes it so ironic that . . .

(3) Philosophy is a *gut.* Practically no one realizes that philosophy is easy—you'd have to *take a philosophy course* to figure *that* out. The reason it's so easy is that it's so impossible. Every little crappy idea you come up with will get you a ticker-tape parade through Greece, if you don't have the sense to keep it to yourself.

After all, philosophy is the only subject that directly addresses the biggest issues facing our world. Its stance on these issues is something like, "Who cares if our discipline has accomplished absolutely nothing in its entire history—we can still go around saying we're 'gadflies' and annoying the hell out of everyone."

REQUIRED VOCABULARY FOR CAPT. PHILOSOPHY AND HIS CREW

Necessary: True in all possible universes—even ones in which there are 3 suns in the sky and man evolved from the pineapple. As it turns out, the one and only necessary truth is the following:

"In 1964, a curious-looking, mop-topped quartet of Liverpudlians scored their first States hit with a harmonica-driven ditty called 'Love Me Do,' kicking off a musical revolution that would forever change the face of rock and roll."

Ethics: The study of good and bad. Today's most hotly debated ethical theory: God and the Devil arm wrestle for mankind's eternal souls. God's stronger, but the Devil keeps lifting his elbow off the table and 'psyching' Him out by grunting really loud.

Political philosophy: Addresses the fundamental problems posed by the State. For example, as Jean-Jacques Rousseau wrote in his *Second Discourse,* "Freakin' taxes goin' through the *roof* this year! Shoot me, dammit, *shoot me* if you ever hear me talkin' 'bout votin' Democrat again. Jimmy Carter, you can just *kiss my fat blue-collar ass,* fellah."

Existentialism: Imagine if you *always* felt like you do when you take a sip from what you think is a glass of milk and it turns out to be orange juice. *Blecccchhh!*

Epistemology: A bunch of hand-wringing about the fact that we don't know anything, and, moreover, we don't even *know* we don't know anything. (Most agree that we *do* know that we don't even know we don't know we don't know anything. This is crucial.)

Hedonism: The theory that people ought to seek their own pleasure. Hedonists have been known to go through an entire bag of Ruffles in one sitting, to watch cable for 10 hours straight, and to have sex with their spouses in weird places, like the kitchen.

Relativism: The position that the world can be different for different people; i.e., what is accepted warmly in one culture may be taboo in another. Relativists are troubled by what appear to be absolute cultural constants: holding food, clothing, and shelter as good, and being hit with a bat, being cut with a knife, and being shot with a gun as evil.

Induction: Reasoning based on experience, as when one figures that the sun has come up every day in the past, so it will come up tomorrow, too. Unfortunately, philosophers have found no logical justification for this. We advise you to get your affairs in order.

COURSES

PHILOSOPHY 146: Metaphysics—OOOOOH!

Metaphysics is the "neatest" *and* least possible part of philosophy. It deals with all the *really* big questions, questions bigger than life itself (but smaller than you'd expect after all the hype). Let us explore each one of them in turn.

Is There a God?

Shhhh! Land sakes, *of course* there's a God! If there's no God, aren't people crazy to build all those churches for "no one"? Isn't the Bible awfully long for a book written by "no one"? And is it "no one" that makes your

prayers come true? Well, all of this makes sense as soon as you substitute "God" for "no one." "Jesus" works, too.

Are There Physical Objects?

Ha ha ha! How silly! *Yes*, for Pete's sake. Bang your head against a brick wall and try telling me *that's* your imagination, if you're not crying too hard to talk. Besides, if there were no physical objects, there'd be nothing to stop you from falling right through the floor and busting your head open in the basement. But here you are, reading peacefully. Ergo . . .

Is There Such a Thing as Good and Evil?

Give me a break. Ever met a *nice* guy? Ever met a *mean* guy? You tell *me* if there's such a thing as good and evil.

Is It Possible to Know Something?

No. It is *never* possible to know something; in fact, we cannot even define what it would be to have true, complete knowledge of anything. Except your *name.* And your *age.* And your *address.* And your favorite food, your job, your friends, and *many, many* other things.

PHILOSOPHY 8: Great Philosophical Thinkers

We shall now explore the work of the four brilliant, ground-breaking philosophers who are given the most attention at Harvard. What follows is difficult material, so skip it if you like.

Wittgenstein

In his own day, young Ludwig Wittgenstein strutted around town like a man who knew he was *the* hardest philosopher ever. Since then, legions of lesser philosophers have dedicated their entire careers to making heads or tails of even his simplest writings, for example, his children's book.

There is an unspoken rule in the Harvard philosophy department that Wittgenstein's writings must be mentioned once in every lecture but must never be discussed. At lectures for the course entitled "The Philosophy of Wittgenstein," the professor just steps to the podium, shrugs his shoulders, and glances at his watch for an hour.

The most important thing about Wittgenstein's work is that nobody has ever understood a single line of it, not even his psychiatrist (Rogerian therapy, once a week for 3 years). Wittgenstein's philosophy is just like poetry—it's boring, it means whatever the experts say it does, and half the time it doesn't even rhyme.

Here's an example from the famous *Tractatus Logico-Philosophicus* (Latin for "Logisch-Philosophische Abhandlung"), in which Wittgenstein famously proves that all philosophy is bullshit:

2.12	The world is everything that is the case.
2.121	The world is the totality of facts, not of things.
2.122	so much depends
2.13	upon
2.2	a red wheel
2.3	barrow
2.31	glazed with rain
2.311	water
2.32	beside the white
2.321	chickens.

Notice Wittgenstein's precise numbering system, which doesn't mean jack.

The other thing to know is that Wittgenstein changed his mind a lot. As we have just seen, he started out trying to prove that philosophy was bullshit. He succeeded at proving this, and realized the next day that

Wittgenstein pauses mid-lecture to clear his throat, and he coughs up the entire Universe.

his proof, being philosophy itself, was bullshit, too. This meant, of course, that philosophy was okay after all.

Buoyed by a new confidence, Wittgenstein quit his day job and wrote a very long and influential hard book called *Philosophical Investigations.* Those few who have read the book agree that—you guessed it—it's bullshit.

Kant

Immanuel Kant is most famous for his great contribution to the study of ethics, which is: "What if *everyone* did that?" Kant developed this theory as a direct challenge to Hegel's "If Mom says no, ask Grandma" dialectic.

Kant's other major achievement was to claim that it is possible to "just *know*" certain things, without ever having been told. Some types of knowledge, he says, are built into the way the mind works, and indeed into the very structure of logical thought. As examples he gives, "My penis is just a *little* bigger than average," and, "I look better if I comb my hair over my bald spot."

Descartes

René Descartes was the greatest philosopher ever to be a victim of a typographical error. His most famous deduction, "I think, therefore I am," is obviously missing the word "smart" at the end. And he must have been smart to have come up with modern philosophy's grooviest idea: What if life is just a dream?

Wrote Descartes, "I can suppose that everything I perceive around me is only a figment of my imagination. The body I have always thought myself to inhabit may be of a quite different sort, or it may not exist at all. My entire life up to this point may exist only as a dream."

To test this hypothesis, Descartes pinched himself. He didn't wake up, so he stuck a fork into his hand. He still didn't wake up, so he set off a really annoying alarm clock. This time, he woke up. As it turned out, reality was just like Descartes's dream world had been, with one exception: In reality Descartes was 4 feet tall, unemployed, and married to a potted palm. The great philosopher soon died from an overdose of sleeping pills.

Mill

John Stuart Mill spent an unhealthy portion of his time posing hypothetical questions designed to crumble even the strongest conscience. See how you'd deal with this example:

Mill: Suppose, for a moment, that you are driving a trolley car, and ahead of you are 5 men, trapped on the tracks. The car has no brakes. You cannot stop, but you can switch to a track with only one man on it. What do you do?

Conscience: I switch tracks and kill one man. After all, 5 lives are better saved than one.

Mill: A fine answer, but there is one thing you ignore. That *man* . . . is *your mother.*

PHILOSOPHY 120: Why?

You may be familiar with the story of the philosophy final on which the only question was, "Why?" Legend has it that one student, instead of scribbling furiously for 3 hours like everyone else, just wrote, "Why not?" and got an A. The truth is that the student wrote, "Why not, asshole?" and got kicked out of school.

But it is important for you to know that "Why?" is the hottest, most controversial topic in philosophy today. Philosophers are largely divided into 3 camps: "To get to the other side," "To keep their pants up," and, "Hey, if you were that ugly, you'd settle for a donkey yourself!"

PSYCHOLOGY

It's commonly thought that those who study psychology are more messed up than the average person, implying that knowing a lot about something can draw you in and make you *more* susceptible to its dangers. This might be why so many football-field injuries are incurred by actual professional football players, or why so many plane crashes claim pilots as victims.

On the other hand, maybe you just have to be crazy to think that psychology isn't a bunch of goofball mumbo-jumbo. But let us not be so quick to judge . . .

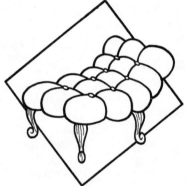

TERMS TO INTERNALIZE INTO YOUR SUBCONSCIOUS

Psychoanalysis: This Freudian method of therapy draws on notions of unconscious conflict and psychosexual development, and, yes, it's the one with the couch.

Id: In Freudian theory, the individual's striving for immediate biological satisfaction, regardless of costs. The line in *Risky Business* where the guy says, "Sometimes you just gotta say what the fuck" is about as close as you can get to describing the id without giving it away.

Ego: Freud's second stage of individual development, when the id reacts to the demands of reality. For instance, a child no longer wishes to own the moon, settling for a BMW, a house in the suburbs, and 2.3 children of its own.

Superego: Freud's final stage of development, when the internalized rules of society are represented by reaction patterns within the ego, which control desires with guilt. E.g., you would kill your next-door neighbors if you didn't feel bad about bothering an overworked police force.

Displacement: Occasionally a person will become angry and punch a wall or kick over his desk. Unless the wall or desk was asking for it, this is displacement.

Classical conditioning: Famously exemplified by Pavlov's dogs, who trained Pavlov to ring a bell whenever they drooled.

Reinforcement: A beaming smile or a stinging slap in the face. It all depends.

Metacognition: Psychologists are unsure what this term means,

though they have a strong feeling that it is very important. Research teams at the top universities in the world are racing to uncover its definition.

Encoding specificity principle: You are most likely to recall something if you are in a situation similar to when it first entered your memory. If someone kicks you in the ribs, you are most likely to remember the incident the *next* time he kicks you in the ribs, especially if he's wearing the same jackboots.

Psychopharmacology: It seems that drugs affect human emotions and behavior in different ways. At the moment, psychopharmacologists are experimenting to see whether if you give people enough nicotine they will act and feel like a tar-covered lung.

Psychopathology: The study of crazy people. Attempts to find out whether they behave that way because they think it's cute.

COURSES

PSYCHOLOGY 1: Introduction to Psychology
  This class gets you acquainted with the key figures in the study of what goes on in the human skull. Let's meet the nutzoids who made it happen!

Sigmund Freud: A strong man with a stronger sexual appetite, Freud is

considered the father of psychology; his numerous illegitimate children went on to make great discoveries in the field. Similar things can be said about Freud's protégé, **Carl Jung**— he *wishes*.

Pavlov: This pioneer of behavioral psychology conditioned the general public to think of gross dogs drool-

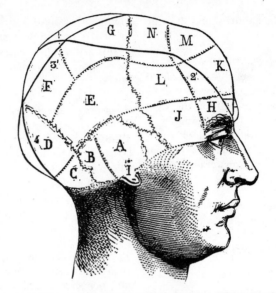

The human brain and its contents: (A) Mussolini's birthday, (B) winning Pac-Man patterns, (C) recipe for Red Velvet Cake, (D) "dead baby" jokes, (E) cuss words, (F) Keats's "On First Looking Into Chapman's Homer," (G) correct spelling of "separate," (H) how to drive stick, (I) skeet-shooting trivia, (J) where I was when Roy Orbison died, (K) sex fantasies about weathermen, (L) suppressed memories of previous life as a sea cucumber, (M) the sum of 5.1 and 33.4, (N) the heady smell of fresh roasted mung beans.

ing all over slabs of meat whenever someone mentions psychology.

B.F. Skinner: A brilliant and terrifying Harvard professor who brought a lead pipe to every lecture in case anyone needed "conditioning." Skinner introduced the notion that you can talk to students until you're blue in the face, but it takes a good whack in the solar plexus to smarten them up.

Noam Chomsky: A linguist, Chomsky enjoyed making fun of the way people spoke, cruelly caricaturing even the slightest lisps and stutters.

Jean Piaget: Contradicting the cruel, animal-torturing B.F. Skinner, Piaget argued that man develops first by annoyingly *imitating* others, but after getting the shit kicked out of him soon learns to quietly *represent* himself. With such fancy terms as *sensory motor control* and *object permanence*, the Frenchman proved that he was nobody's fool.

Erik Erikson: Gave psychology "The Eight Stages of Man," which he claimed arose from different crises, including: the loss of *identity*, the search for *intimacy*, and the development of *acne*. Erikson once said, "In youth you find out who you care to be. In young adulthood you learn whom you care to be with. In adulthood, you learn who cares for the garbage, and on what day they come to take it." Ironically, the psychoanalyst made his discoveries during his own final stage, *senility*; Erik Erikson currently believes that he is a Viking.

PSYCHOLOGY 165: Abnormal Psychology
This course considers wacky case studies—the stuff of which psychology is made. It concludes with a trip to the local loony bin, chaperoned by none other than Charlie Manson himself. Have yourself a look through our files . . .

I. The Déjà Vu Guy.

Mr. Smith (not his real name) experienced constant déjà vu. Everything he did, every place he visited, seemed somehow familiar. Even his déjà vu experiences themselves felt as though they had happened once before. One day Mr. Smith decided that he had to do something to convince himself that he was living his life for the first time. What can I do, he thought, that I couldn't *possibly* have done before?

He took out the ammonia from under the sink and drank it down. Its taste was very familiar, as was the sensation of his heart stopping, his consciousness fading, and his very life ending. His last words, spoken at the moment of death, were, "Weren't we in the third grade together or something, my sweet Lord?"

II. The Reverse-Paranoia Lady.

Mrs. Smith (not her real name) was a reverse paranoiac—she suffered under the delusion that she was out to get everyone around her. Believing her walking stick to conceal a deadly blade and her purse to contain a loaded pistol, Mrs. Smith would stroll about her neighborhood, offering people fresh-baked cookies, asking after their families, and rationalizing that her infinite kindness and generosity was just a facade.

III. The Obsessive-Compulsive Lady.

Mrs. Smith (not her real name) was obsessive-compulsive. On a typical day, she would wash her hands over 500,000 times. To cure Mrs. Smith of this disorder, her psychiatrist left her alone, locked in a comfortable room, for a period of 24 hours. The room contained no source of running water. When the psychiatrist went to retrieve Mrs. Smith, he found her sitting in the middle of the floor, her hands thickly coated with dripping, reeking, putrid filth.

IV. The Multiple Guy.

Mr. Smith (not his real name) had a single personality, but multiple appearances. "Joey" had a mole on his right cheek, "Frank" had a mole on his left cheek, and "Larry" had no mole at all. It is hard to describe how disturbing, how *chilling*, it was to be talking to Frank when suddenly, without any warning, Joey would take his place.

V. The Oedipal Guy.

Mr. Jones (real name Smith) wanted to kill his father and have sex with his mother, so he did. Now he is the sanest person on earth.

PSYCHOLOGY 200x: Individual Research

This course gives psych majors the opportunity to find out whether what they've been learning in the classroom applies to the real world. This usually means going to the freshman dining hall with a stack of "scientific" questionnaires, getting as many frosh as possible to fill them out while they eat, licking the tuna casserole off the completed surveys, and then compiling the results. As you can imagine, the psych major ends up with an intimate, deeply probing profile of his subjects, as on the following page:

PSYCHOLOGY QUESTIONNAIRE

Thank you for taking the time to fill out this questionnaire. Please respond thoughtfully and seriously to the five (5) questions below. You need not sign your name. The results will be used to prepare a senior thesis in social psychology.

QUESTION 1: Please list the ten (10) qualities that you believe are most important to a friendship.

I don't know about this "friendship" stuff, but last night I dreamed about a great big PENIS entering a great big VAGINA. What do you make of that, Doctor Freud?

QUESTION 2: Which of these qualities apply to your relationship with the person you consider your best friend?

All of them. NO, you idiot, only SOME of them. NO, both of you guys are wrong —NONE of them. Hey, sorry this answer is so confusing - I've got a split personality!

QUESTION 3: Describe yourself with a list of five (5) qualities.

Short, French, wear a funny hat, always have my hand in my shirt, got screwed over at the Battle of Waterloo.

QUESTION 4: Describe your best friend with a list of five (5) qualities.

I can't answer that. How do you expect me to write with a straight-jacket on?

QUESTION 5: If you could change any of your best friend's qualities, which would you change and how?

ahhh, ahhhh, AHHHH - oh, sorry, I was fantasizing about my mommy!

RELIGION

Most religion majors at Harvard first got interested in the subject when they saw *The Exorcist* in junior high and fell in love with the idea of a job where you get paid to watch adolescent girls writhe around on their beds and talk dirty. Harvard's religion department caters to the career-oriented nature of its students, with its courses including practical information such as how to deal with hecklers during your sermon, and whether the rabbi or the priest should get top billing at an interfaith marriage.

As in any largely pre-professional major, cutthroat competition abounds. For example, since religion majors' piety is graded on a curve, students immediately start cracking jokes and making fart noises whenever one of their classmates tries to pray. Or if one student is giving confession, others will stand right outside and make eerie moaning sounds, hardly noticeable at first, but gradually getting louder and louder until it's impossible to ignore. "Larry . . . *ahhhhhhhmmmm* . . . remember me? . . . *ohhhhhhmmmm* . . . you said if I told you my sins I wouldn't go to Hell, Larry . . . *ahhhhhhhhmmmm* . . . you lied, Larry . . . *ohhhhhhhhhmmmm* . . . and now I'm back . . . MUHAHAHAHAHAHAH!" If this doesn't work, they'll lob a few stink bombs into the confessional and hide behind the altar.

Don't get the idea that there isn't some real spirituality going on here, though—in fact, by the time they graduate, most religion majors are devout followers of several different faiths. Granted, this also looks pretty good on a resume . . .

THE WORDS OF GOD

Atheism: The belief that the Bible was written as a novel, that Jesus was simply a good actor, and that *if* it turns out there is a Heaven, they probably won't check too close anyway.

Agnosticism: "Acknowledging the possibility" of God's existence. Acknowledging is similar to worshipping, but instead of saying prayers and singing hymns, you just look up at the sky and say, "Maybe you is, and maybe you ain't."

Animism: The belief that all things in the world are imbued with souls. In 1969, the State of California recognized the first marriage performed by an animist minister, between a rock and a sweet potato.

Transubstantiation: The Catholic doctrine that bread and wine are changed into the body and blood of Jesus. There's a kid at every Catholic school who doesn't believe this until he goes home one Sunday after Mass and throws up a beard and sandals.

Reincarnation: The notion that after death, the souls of human beings live on in other forms. If you're wondering, John Paul I was reincarnated as a big plate of matzoh ball soup in a hungry rabbi's kitchen.

COURSES

RELIGION 1: Basic Concepts of Religion

Praying

The most important thing the religion department teaches you is how to pray to God. First, place your fingers at your temples and concentrate very hard on Heaven. Then, think the following:

"Thank you I love you thank you I love you thank you I love you thank you I love you thank you I love you thank you I love you."

Then open your eyes, rub your noggin, and say, "Whew."

God

One man claims to have actually met God after buying a dollar's

Sure, it's impolite to point, but that never stopped the Lord of All Creation.

worth of cherrystone clams from an office vending machine. Here we ask him about his experience:

Lampoon: So what'd He look like?

Man: Pretty much like you'd expect: white guy, gray hair, slightly overweight. Kind of like Archie Bunker, but holier.

Lampoon: How about Jesus?

Man: Oh, you mean "Meathead." The Polish guy with long brown hair, right?

But a question still rankles: If God is immortal—never ages—then why is He an old man? Why not youthful? Wouldn't it be better if He was in his prime: tall, athletic, deep tan, beaming, gap-toothed smile? In fact, if He's truly immortal, shouldn't He still be a newborn baby? A precocious child, of course; able to crawl, speak several words of English, and set a bush afire by clapping.

The Devil

Learning how to deal with the Devil is also very important to your education, but for Pete's sake, don't go messin' about with black magic and things beyond the ken a' mortal man . . .

The way they work is this: The Devil makes a pact with some guy who wants power or love or whatever and the guy trades him his soul. Which would be fine, except the Devil always has to welsh on his side of the deal.

For example, the guy asks for Victoria Principal. Fair enough. He wants the best. But the Devil figures he heard "Victoria Principull," who turns out to be pretty much the same, only she has slightly wider nostrils. Or, in another instance, the guy says the Devil can have his soul, but in return he wants to play the violin and gain the power to write things for the Joffrey Ballet which would make clumsy, knock-kneed people feel beautiful. The Devil says

fine, and takes the guy's soul, and gives him the powers of song and dance like he asked. Then he turns around, and *screws* the guy.

RELIGION 120: Comparative Religions

There's a vast number of religions in the world, but they all have one basic message: There is a God, and she's Black.

Everything else is just icing on the cake, as the following survey should demonstrate.

Judaism: There are several varieties of Judaism—Reform, Conservative,

"God is different to each one of us, but we all agree that Jesus is this dumb old stick."

Extremely Conservative, and Roman Catholic. As a result, the distinctions can be confusing. For instance:

First Guy: Lenny's a Hassidic Jew.
Second Guy: (*pause*) "That's bad, right?"

Catholicism: You've seen them in those church movies, in confession, stepping into the right half of a converted telephone booth with a sliding panel in the middle, and writing on a slip of paper, "Bless me Father ... I have sinned," then giving the paper to a man who types it up on a computer screen and has it faxed to Akron, Ohio, where it is bounced off a satellite dish.

The dish retrieves signals from confession boxes all over America and Western Europe and assimilates them into a clear signal which is broadcast via milk delivery truck back to the left half of the confession booth and into a small hearing aid in the priest's right ear. Then the priest says, "When was the last time you came to confession, my pet?" and without missing a beat, slaps that dang sinner across the face.

Meanwhile, there are women called nuns who marry God. Which gives rise to this question: If they divorce Him, do they get to keep half the universe?

Quakers are into asceticism, religious freedom, and putting belt buckles on their hats. Their beliefs? Suffice it to say that there are solid theological underpinnings to all the ridiculous Quaker nonsense. Their clothes are plain because their bodies are frilly and garish; their life-styles are strict because their afterlives will be spent gorging on sausage in a meat-filled garden of earthly pleasures.

Franciscans take a vow of absolute silence, then devote the rest of their lives to listening to Judas Priest at full volume. One breakaway sect of Franciscans uses a modified version of the vow of silence in which they can talk, but they can't ever tell anyone to shut up.

Buddhism: Buddhists are interested in learning to control their bodies. One master practitioner has, through years of fierce training, so completely mastered his heart rate that he has been buried alive 43 times.

Christian Science: Christian scientists distrust modern medicine and do not believe in combatting even grave illnesses by taking drugs. Christian scientists are very, very, very healthy people.

Mormons: Mormon men are allowed by their religion to keep as many wives as they want, but usually they try and keep it down to a couple thousand or so. Mormons like their situation and work together as a cohesive weirdo family unit. Here is a typical evening at a Mormon dinner table:

Wife 1: Hello, hon.
Wife 2: How was your day, sweet-heart?
Wife 3: Hi, how ya doin', dear.
Husband: Wife 76—pass the turkey!

Hinduism: Hindus frequently en-counter a religious dilemma: They respect cows as sacred animals, but they love a good steak. Also, that red dot you always see on the foreheads of Hindu people turns out to be a birthmark after all.

Cults and Sects: Some cults worship terrifying mythical beasts and de-monic creatures, which, upon a whim, they can summon to wreak havoc. Other cults are even cooler, like the one surrounding the mes-sage you hear if you play "Stairway to Heaven" backwards—namely, the Bible. Here are some other neat cults:

Scientology: Scientologists follow the edicts set forth by erstwhile sci-ence fiction author L. Ron Hubbard in his famous cult novel, the Talmud. L. Ron Hubbard has since left home, and disappeared without a trace, leaving only that suspicious-looking lump wiggling around under the bedsheets.

Hare Krishna: Krishnas hang around airports, beating their gongs and cymbals, and hitting people up for music-lesson money. The leader of the Krishnas owns 96 Rolls-Royce automobiles, but as yet has only been able to acquire four or five little Rolls-Royce people to drive them.

RELIGION 200: Religion and Popular Culture
In 1966 John Lennon set off a huge commotion by telling the press that the Beatles were more popular than Jesus. Fans demanded an ex-planation, and religious people de-manded an apology. Lennon, reasoning that he had done nothing wrong just as long as what he said was correct, hired Gallup to take a poll.

Gallup's first task was to discern what Lennon meant by "popular." To find out, they polled Lennon. One hundred percent of those polled responded, "Figger it out f' yer bleedin' selves, ya queers."

So Gallup prepared a question-naire and sent it out to a statistically significant portion of the world's population: one man and one woman for every possible combina-tion of hair color and eye color. Here's how it turned out:

Questions	*Responses*
1) Suppose you had a secret that you wanted to tell, but only to someone you really trusted. Would you tell the Beatles, or Jesus?	Beatles—10% Jesus—12% "Secrets? Goodness, I don't know any secrets."—78%

Questions	Responses
2) Suppose you had two pieces of cake, one delicious and the other only good. Would the Beatles, or Jesus, get the delicious piece?	Beatles—6% Jesus—5% "Cake . . . Jeez, I'll have to check the pantry . . . would a couple Twinkies do?"—89%
3) Suppose a terrorist gave you a gun and said you had to kill either Jesus or the Beatles, or else he would kill both himself. Who would you kill?	Beatles—11% Jesus—8% "I'd shoot the terrorist."—81%
4) Suppose Jesus and the Beatles were running against each other for President of the United States. Who would get your vote?	Beatles—4% Jesus—9% "I vote Republican."—87%
5) If you could have the autograph of either the Beatles or Jesus, *but not both,* whose would you get?	Beatles—12% Jesus—11% "I don't collect autographs, but once I saw Milton Berle at the airport."—77%
6) If the Beatles and Jesus had a religious battle, who would win?	Beatles—8% Jesus—64% "Well, if the Beatles don't believe in Jesus, does he die?"—28%
7) If Jesus and the Beatles had a musical battle, who would win?	Beatles—60% Jesus—10% "What do I know by Jesus?"—30%
8) All right, who's more popular?	Beatles—100% Jesus—0%

RELIGION 156: The Spiritual Life of Children

Children, though slightly more finite than the rest of us, often have deeply insightful conceptions of the infinite. Consider the following pictures, created by a second-grade class when asked to draw God.

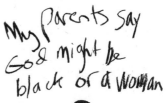

My Parents say God might be black or a woman

I'm GOD. Who the hell are you?

God is like My Uncle Ray He is scary and mean and has cancer.

GOD IS EVERY WHERE EVEN IN MY POTTY.

VISUAL AND ENVIRONMENTAL STUDIES (V.E.S.)

The V.E.S. concentration is composed of studio art (drawing, painting, sculpture), the photographic arts (photography, motion pictures), design science (graphic design, environmental design, architecture), and, until recently, French things (French artists, French culture, French accents) as well. The "French things" portion was eliminated by the "Fellini Clause," enacted when it was discovered that legitimate art could occasionally be produced outside of France.

With the deletion of the "French things" portion of the department, the name of the entire concentration was changed from "*Vraiment, Écoutez-moi, Serieusement!*" (trans. "Why won't anyone listen to me?") to the current "Visual and Environmental Studies." There is no truth to the rumor that V.E.S. stands for "Very Easy Subject." Okay, maybe just a little truth.

The name "visual and *environmental* studies" connotes some relation to the earth-sciences concentration. Do not be confused by this. The "environmental" exists solely to placate those who might be upset with paying exorbitant sums of money for something that could easily be learned independently over spring break. This feeling was summed up beautifully by Mrs. Ella Wishnatski, whose son was a V.E.S. graduate in 1989: "I ain't paying eighty G's for my son to graduate in 'art!'" Unfortunately, Mrs. Wishnatski, you are.

While the once-mighty department has suffered a steady decline in enrollment since the Surgeon General warned of the dangers of excessive smoking, the V.E.S. concentration remains steadfast in its commitment to the artistic way of life, embracing many disciplines:

Drawing/Painting

If you can draw or paint well before you enroll in the course, you will get a good grade. If you can't draw or paint to save your life, you will only get a B+. If you try to draw something that looks real, you are in trouble. If you render instead "The Way Love Feels," you are in good shape.

Photography

If you put an infinite number of monkeys in a room with an infinite number of typewriters, you would find the stench quite unbearable. Likewise, if you, or any other simian creature, were to take a camera and shoot such a vast number of photographs, some of them would be very artistically relevant. Quantity = Quality.

Graphic Design

Remember third-grade art class, when you had to paste together collages of interesting words and images cut out of colorful magazines and newspapers with those dinky metal scissors that had dried glue all over them? All of that has changed in college-level graphic design courses: you can now use an X-Acto knife.

Film Theory

Hitchcock, despite being interesting and entertaining, is a "good" director. Godard and Truffaut are French—enough said. Enjoyable films "lack the artistic and cinematic creativity of the masters."

The words "plot," "storyline," and "action" are transcended by the art film. The use of symbolism and metaphor replace and make obsolete the need for these cheap and tawdry concessions to the Hollywood mainstream. If you understand the film, then it is not art.

SOME V.E.S. TERMS ONE OUGHT TO LEARN AND FORGET IMMEDIATELY TO AVOID BEING SLAPPED

-esque, -ian: Appended to any name, any term, it becomes more descriptive, more utile, more pretentious. E.g.: Dreyeresque, Godardian, Hitchcockesque, Rolltopdesque, Iwentskian.

Diane Arbus: All black-and-white photographs of human subjects remind you of the work of Diane Arbus. Not necessarily true, but a dynamite way to kill half a page while writing a paper.

The Dziga Vertov Group: A socialist group of French filmmakers formed by Jean-Luc Godard. Geniuses, every one of them, *geniuses.*

The "Act of selective framing": This is what gives photographers and filmmakers their "God-like power." It is the skilled employ of this act which makes art films so boring. Use this term as much as possible.

Susan Sontag: A brilliant and insightful film critic. Her bountiful criticism is always correct.

Representational vs. Abstract: Respectively interchangeable with "bad" and "good." E.g.: "That drawing looks too much like something that might actually exist; it's *representational*. I like that sloppy and incomprehensible blot with little scratches and dots on it; it's *abstract*."

COURSES

V.E.S. 200: Introduction to Filmmaking

Do you want to be the next Ingmar Bergman? No? Then how about the one after that? All good "art films" begin with a good "art script." Pay close attention to the symbols of death, evil, and oppression present in the form of garments in the following brilliant piece of screenwriting:

FADE IN:
Interior Billy's Room—Day
Billy wakes up. We meet him for the first time. Billy has been sleeping. (Note: Billy has been sleeping under a large woolen blanket, and is obscured from view from the waist down. He may be nude, but we can't tell, as we can't see him under the blanket. The audience will be suspicious as to whether he is naked or not. The blanket is warm.) Billy is

still tired, so he sleeps some more.
CUT TO:

Interior Billy's Room—Later in the Same Day
We cut back to Billy's room later in the same day. Billy is still asleep. We cut to a wide shot of his room. It is big and messy. It says a lot about Billy; he is six foot three. That is pretty big. Billy is not as messy as his room. There are lots of things on the furniture.
CUT TO:

Exterior, the Street—Day
Billy is not here yet, as he is now cleaning his room.
CUT TO:

Exterior, the Street—Later in the Same Day
Billy walks along the street. He is fully clothed, but he wears only one sock. This is important. We don't

know why. Billy got dressed after he woke up, but we didn't see this. It happened off-camera. (Note: Billy may have been partially clothed when he was under the blanket, but, if so, he was only wearing one sock.)

CUT TO:

Exterior, the Other Street—Day
Billy continues to walk along the street, but it's a different street. (Note: it could be the same street, but it must be a different block, unless it's a little further down on the same block.)

CUT TO:

Exterior, the Same Street—Day
We see the man that is following Billy. He is a large man. (Note: He does not have to be too large.) This man is wearing a hat. This man has a headache. Every time we see this man he has a headache. We don't know why, but it may be because of the hat.

CUT TO:

Exterior, Street—Day
Billy is being followed by the man with the hat. He still wears the hat, but not on his head. His headache is worse. The headache was caused by the hat. The sock is cleverly concealed behind the hat.

CUT TO DREAM SEQUENCE:

Dream Sequence—Day
Billy is now following the man with the hat. Billy is wearing the hat. Billy looks good in the hat. The man's headache is better now. Suddenly the man turns and refuses to walk ahead of Billy, or behind him. He motions that he wishes for Billy to walk beside him and be his friend. The man has no friends. Billy tries to run, but discovers that his knees bend the wrong way. He tries to run but instead falls down and KICKS HIMSELF IN THE GROIN. (Note: special shoes may be worn to protect the actor from kidney damage.)

END DREAM SEQUENCE: CUT TO:

Interior, Billy's Real Room—Day
The room we were in before was not actually Billy's room, but this one is. Billy is here, sleeping. Billy does not awake, as he has died of Kragsmeyer's disease several hours before. He still wears one sock, but in deference to the dead, it is on backwards.

FADE OUT

THE END

VES 223: Advanced Photography

Photography isn't just a way to record the look on Uncle Zeke's face when the belly dancer shows up at his birthday party. Nope, taking snaps can be an art just like everything else. To prove that, here is an award-winning photo project on the following pages, for which the assignment was to "illustrate the power of human emotion." You will notice how the photographer manipulates the subtlest details of lighting, framing, focus, processing, and printing to evoke his chosen emotion.

ANXIETY
By Rockwood Schmeliger

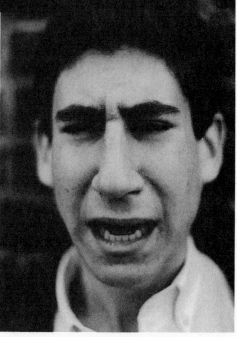

Part
IV

NOW WHAT?

NOW WHAT?!?

Well, that's it.

We've covered everything that you've got to know to graduate from Harvard College, and also a few timeless lessons of life and love that usually take 30-odd years to turn a fresh-faced, cocksure Harvard grad into a hardened, seasoned wino. Though some pages remain unturned, you could close the book right now and your Harvard education would be complete. We extend our heartiest congratulations.

Look in the mirror, Harvard grad, and relish the reflection of your devout commitment and hard work. You are learned, erudite, accomplished—a deserving holder of the diploma at the end of this book. Of course, none of that shows in the mirror.

What *does* show is the Frito crumbs all over your shirt, the cat puke on your shoes, and that counterfeit designer wristwatch you won playing Skee-Ball. The thing says "GOOCHIE" on it, for crying out loud. Your head is a Fort Knox of wisdom, but your pockets are just as empty as they were before you started.

So how about it? Are you ready to get on the phone and use your new credentials to snag the job that will make you a zillionaire? You are? *Go ahead!*

Why aren't you dialing? Is it because you're not cut out for the rich life? Because you're afraid you'd get a swelled head and forget where you came from? Because you couldn't bear to give up your mop, bucket, and half-room apartment in the basement of P.S. 135?

Or is it because you have no freaking idea who to call? Aha!

We admit it. Way back when we promised all the nifty things that a Harvard education would do for you, we weren't completely honest. In fact, it was a crock. The conventional wisdom has got it right—it's not *what* you know, but *who* you know.

What important people *do* you know? You once saw a guy who

looked kind of like Lee Iacocca renting a stack of pornies at the video store? That's just not going to cut it.

Maybe it's *our* fault. We dare not hazard a guess as to how many potential "connections" have kept a wide berth of you just because you had this book in your hands. That's why we've decided to fulfill our original promise and put you where a Harvard grad deserves to be—on top.

Now see what you've won.

YOUR NEW DREAM JOB

You, Dear Reader, have been hired to sell bonds for the Wall Street investment banking firm of Lye, Cheet, Steele & Silverblatt at a starting salary of $150,000. You're expected at nine o'clock sharp on Monday morning.

Report for duty to the New England branch offices, housed in the 200 stories of glass and steel at 44 Bow Street in Cambridge, Massachusetts. Mr. Silverblatt himself will be there to show you around and go over the details of the employee medical, dental, and hair-replacement plans.

There's a corner office waiting for you on the 199th floor, conveniently right down the hall from the racquetball courts, the driving range, the wild game preserve, and the bowling alley with upside-down pins for higher scores. It's just a brief ride in your private glass elevator to the world's only revolving restaurant with a conveyor belt buffet.

Have a seat in your plush recliner, custom-molded to fit the personal curves of your buttocks. Push the black button on the armrest for a vibra-massage and some easy-listening. Push the white button to summon Melanie Griffith, your personal secretary with built-in coffee machine. Push the blue button to conjure up a *Pretty Woman*-style prostitute in less time than it takes to push the yellow button and fill your private Jacuzzi with Evian. But whatever you do, don't push the red button.

You'll have access to a company car (complete with cellular phone with pre-programmed 900 "chat" numbers) as well as a company helicopter (machine guns and rocket launchers). And, of course, you'll be welcome on the annual company vacation to Aruba—that's *planet* Aruba.

But don't think your new job is all fun and games—you've got some very serious responsibilities. Last week, Mr. Silverblatt's yokel cousin died and left him a hog farm. Mr. Silverblatt wants you to get started selling the hogs to his clients as "special limited-issue bonds," at $5,000 a head.

We realize how suddenly all this has come, so we've prepared a little guide to help you adjust to your new role. You can keep it under your blotter and peek at it when nobody's looking.

GUIDE TO YOUR NEW DREAM JOB

What to Say to Your SECRETARY

- "Can't you give a *real* back rub? I'm tense as hell—put some *oomph* into it, for crying out loud!"
- "Christ Almighty, this is lukewarm! If I wanted lukewarm coffee, I'd have said, 'Oh, and Melanie, make it *lukewarm*.' Did I say that? DID I SAY ANYTHING REMOTELY LIKE THAT?!"
- "Here's $500. Now go downtown and buy yourself a *decent* dress, and then I'm gonna watch you throw that potato sack in the incinerator. GO!"

What to Say to Your BOSS

- "Don't worry, sir, it won't happen again. And if it does, I'll cut off my other pinkie."
- "Why, sir, what a beautiful tie! Such fine detail—is each clown playing a different sport?"
- "My, your neck's especially tight today, sir. I'll heat up some oil."

What to Say to Your CLIENTS

- "Well, you can't find an investment that's more . . . uh, bristly . . ."
- "Yes . . . these 'bonds' have the highest USDA—er, I mean, *Standard & Poor* rating."
- "Look, I'm just gonna cut right through the bull for you. Pigs are recession-proof."

Believe it or not, life as a Harvard grad is more than just a dream job. Turn the page to see what else you got for your $7.95 . . .

Pretty sweet, eh? "Aw *heck* yeah," you say, "but what gives? All your books must promise the same job, house, yacht, and potty!" True indeed. We'll worry about that the day we sell the second copy.

Anyway, *you're* all set. You have everything you could possibly want out of life, just as we promised. But it's not over yet. Now we confer upon you the greatest privilege of them all.

We wish there was some way to make this more ceremonial, but that's hard to do in a book. We tried to get the publisher to spring for a little confetti that would fall out on your lap when you turned to this page, but you'll have to settle for this:

Ta-Dah!

Congratulations, Reader. You are the newest member of the world's most exclusive, influential group of men. You've seen their pictures in the newspaper "society column," where they stood out as beacons of gentility amidst the barbarism of Hägar the Horrible and Erma Bombeck. You've heard their names whispered in country club bathrooms by the men who gave you the biggest tips. You've read about them, you've heard about them, and now you're one of them.

Welcome to the Old Boy Network.

The Old Boy Network, until this day, has been composed of these five Harvard graduates, the entire Class of 1687. They have played Presidents and Kings as their pawns for 300 years, and now they invite you to do the same. Picture yourself seated at the head of a groaning oaken table, somewhere fathoms underground, feasting on roast pheasant and truffles while George Bush and Gorby perform an awkward striptease for your entertainment.

What can we say? *You rule the world.* At midnight on the night of the next new moon, tie on a blindfold and stand on the 50-yard line of the local high school football field. After some time—hours, days, or even years—you will feel 3 taps on your left shoulder. At that point you must hold your nose, close your mouth, and breathe out until your ears pop. A ring will be placed on your finger, and you will be taught the secret handshake and the telephone hotline number. We'd tell you *ourselves* . . . if we knew them.

But one thing we *do* know is that when the Gentlemen stand around you, resplendent in their gilted ermine vestments, they'll be wanting to give the once-over to a certain piece of sheepskin . . .

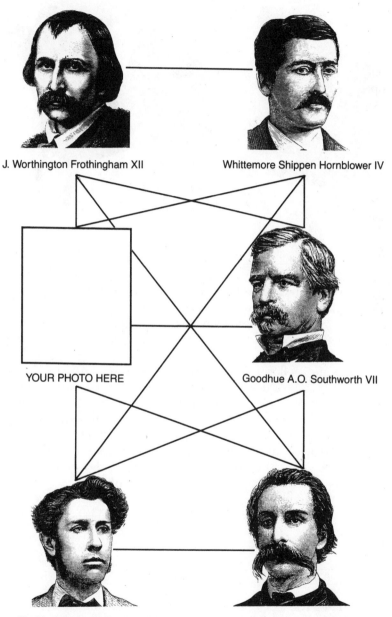

J. Worthington Frothingham XII

Whittemore Shippen Hornblower IV

YOUR PHOTO HERE

Goodhue A.O. Southworth VII

Fitz Mackay-Smith Toynbee Jr.

Odysseus P. Iliadeus MCLVIII

ABOUT YOUR HARVARD DIPLOMA

This Harvard diploma has been around the world seven times. It has the power to bring miraculous good fortune to all who receive it *and* who continue the chain by making ten copies and mailing them off to friends who would also like to blessed with incredibly wonderful luck.

Shortly after following these instructions, a woman from Sydney, Australia, became a near-millionare as the result of a hastily settled lawsuit arising from a car crash that killed her husband and children and left her paralyzed below the eyebrows. A man in Reno, Nevada, who continued the chain awoke the next day to find himself well-rested, refreshed. Another man in Reno, Nevada, who continued the chain began getting slightly better gas mileage, although this might have been because he began to drive only downhill.

Those who ignore these instructions, even if nothing bad actually happens to them, will be nagged by "what if" questions 20 years down the road.

Frequently asked questions about the Harvard diploma:

Is my Harvard diploma authentic?

Yes, your diploma is authentic, in the same way that good Elvis impersonators are authentic—only an expert can spot the difference.

Is my Harvard diploma really made of sheepskin?

It is true that college diplomas once were made from wool and used as warm caps in the winter. Your diploma, however, is made from paper, employing an ecologically sensitive process that uses only the wood from specially selected telephone poles.

Where should I hang my Harvard diploma?

Your diploma should be hung so as to cover the bare spot on your bedroom wall. And while you're at it, get rid of that gauche "Beers of the World" poster.

How should I care for my Harvard diploma?

If your diploma becomes stained, rub briskly with a cloth using a non-abrasive liquid cleanser. Never use harsh detergents or steel wool. Always apply a heavy sunscreen to the diploma before taking it outdoors; otherwise, some blanching may result. Store in a warm, dry place, but avoid bodily orifices.

Why does my dog growl at my Harvard diploma and then hide in the broom closet and whine?

Your dog is probably used to being the sole object of your family's affection and may regard the new diploma as a competitor for your love and attention. Reassure your dog by showering him with praise and repeatedly doing that trick where you pull out a quarter from behind his ear.

On the other hand, your dog may just be hinting that the diploma is hung a smidgen off to the left.

Should my Harvard diploma be counted in the next U.S. Census?

Yes. Your diploma is properly counted as a Hispanic male, age 24.

Are there any special safety instructions regarding my Harvard diploma that I should be aware of?

YOUR DIPLOMA SHOULD ALWAYS BE USED UNDER THE CLOSE SUPERVISION OF AN ADULT. Should an accident occur causing the diploma to become lodged in someone's throat, firmly grasp the victim around the waist from behind and, with hands clasped together, repeatedly squeeze in the area of the diaphragm with a quick, jerky motion until the diploma is dislodged. Do not operate heavy machinery after hanging up your diploma, as white-collar work is more pleasant and usually pays better.

Harvard

At Cambridge in the Comm

The President and Fellows of
Consent of the Honorable and
and acting on the recommen
and Sciences, ha

the degree of

cum laude in

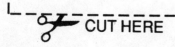

University

onwealth of *Massachusetts*

Harvard College, with the
Reverend Board of Overseers
dation of the Faculty of Arts
ve conferred on

Bachelor of Arts

General Studies

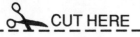

In witness whereof, by auth
have hereunder placed our
University on this thirty-sec
year of our Lord nineteen hu
the Harvard Lampoon the

President

Dean of the Faculty

ority duly committed us, we
names and the seal of the
ond day of Octember in the
ndred and ninety-one and of
one hundred and fifteenth.

Dean of the College

Grand Generalissimo

ABOUT THE AUTHORS

Jon Beckerman is trading in his dingus for a Cadillac-ac-ac-ac-ac-ac.

Robinson Everett, the bastard son of a hundred maniacs, currently works as an intern for *Spy* magazine.

Matthew Moehlman is known around campus as a coltish roustabout with a freakishly huge and dandified upper body.

Brian Reich is identifiable by the dense colony of bunions and corns which obscure his otherwise strikingly handsome facial features.

Jeffrey Schaffer is one of the last of a dying breed: someone who knows being a decent human being is more important than being quick with a joke.

Danny O'Keefe is insane.

(*l to r*) Jeff Schaffer, Jon Beckerman, Matt Moehlman, Robinson "Penn" Everett, Brian Reich, Danny "Teller" O'Keefe

Subscribe to the *Harvard Lampoon*

The *Harvard Lampoon*, founded in 1876, is the nation's oldest humor magazine. The *Lampoon* publishes five issues a year and produces a nationally distributed book or magazine parody every summer. Famous *Lampoon* alumni include John Updike, Robert Benchley, George Plimpton, William Randolph Hearst, George Santayana, Fred Gwynne, the Aga Khan, and Dr. Kenneth C. Keller. Recent grads have gone on to write for "Saturday Night Live," "Late Night with David Letterman," "The Simpsons," "Married With Children," "In Living Color," and *National Lampoon*.

SUBSCRIPTIONS

One Year (5 issues)	$15
Two Years (10 issues)	$30
Lifetime Subscription (15 issues)	$45

Send your name, address, and check to:

Book Subscription Offer
The Harvard Lampoon
44 Bow Street
Cambridge, MA 02138